D1525080

Wanting You

A Small Town Romance

Book 3

Connor Brothers series

By Leah J. Busboom

Dedication

To all of you who enjoy reading a delightful, romantic story just like me.

To my amazing husband—I couldn't do this without your love and support.

"All I ever wanted from you was to know that I was wanted *by* you . . ."
—Richelle E. Goodrich, *Smile Anyway*

Table of Contents

Chapter One

Jacob

"Welcome, gentlemen!" John Vandervoldt's booming voice echoes around the front porch as he motions for us to come inside. He's a tall, stately looking gentleman with a shock of gray hair and an understated demeanor that doesn't hint as to the size of his bank account. Mr. Vandervoldt is one of Connor's Grove's best-known and most well-respected citizens. He owns the only lumberyard in town and is involved in numerous civic activities, including acting as president of the Chamber of Commerce.

Luke, Tom, Shorty, and I pause in the entry, removing our construction boots in case they have dirt on them. The house looks immaculate, almost as if no one lives here. Connor Construction is demolishing an old utility building and putting up a new carriage house at the back of the property. Luke is the foreman of our small crew. Tom, Shorty, and I are the worker bees—we've become a well-oiled machine after several months of working together.

I've been helping my brother Max, who owns and operates the company, since I was laid off from my job in Minneapolis last fall. Working a manual labor job like construction is a great change of pace and has helped me hone muscles that I never thought possible after working a desk job for several years.

Luke rolls the blueprints out on the dining room table. "We plan on tearing down the shed today. Building materials are being delivered tomorrow, so hopefully we can get started on the new carriage house right away," Luke explains to Mr. Vandervoldt as they pore over the plans.

The Vandervoldts live in a spacious yet modest home. Nothing flashy or extravagant. A painting hanging over the sofa catches my eye and I walk closer. Its vibrant colors and edgy design draw you in—an intriguing depiction of wild horses conveyed through an explosion of turbulent colors. With its thick paint and luminous glow, the painting is alive with chaos and emotion. The figures aren't crisp or well defined—like you're looking at them through a fog.

"My granddaughter painted that." Mr. Vandervoldt comes to stand beside me as we gaze at the artwork. His voice reveals that he adores both artwork and artist.

I'm not familiar with all the Vandervoldts, but I went to school with some of them. I wonder which granddaughter he's referring to. "She's very talented."

Glowing with pride, Mr. Vandervoldt says, "She is. I'm actually building the carriage house so she can live there. It'll be a great spot for her to paint." *Not the starving artist type, then.* I feel my esteem for the painting's creator drop a few inches. Mr. Vandervoldt turns to Luke. "I'd like my granddaughter's input on the blueprints as well. Maybe one of you boys can review them with her. She's around here somewhere. I'll send her out to see you."

The crew exchanges disgruntled looks at the prospect of another person's input on the design. It's difficult enough working with married couples and obtaining consensus. What's it going to be like getting a granddaughter and grandfather to agree? And why is her grandfather building the place for her? I wrinkle my nose at the prospect of working with a spoiled rich girl.

Mr. Vandervoldt points us to the dilapidated-looking shed that sits near the far end of their sprawling two-acre lot. Even though it's early spring, the yard is magnificent, with giant oak trees just starting to bud and neatly manicured grass just beginning to turn green. This parcel of land is huge compared to the lots in the newer subdivisions springing up around Connor's Grove.

With an agreed-to plan for demolition, Mr. Vandervoldt confirms that we can get started right away. He instructs us on how

8

to enter the grounds through a side gate, where we can access the jobsite via a dirt road stretching along the east side of the property. We leave, anxious to get the project underway. But I'm not especially anxious to meet the granddaughter.

~*~

The old utility shed is sturdier than it looks. We all assumed that the ramshackle structure would topple over with one swing of the hammer. Not true. Tom, Shorty, and I are sweating our butts off ripping this old building down board by board. Luke's abandoned us to go into town to check on the delivery of the building materials.

"Man, why are we having 80-degree temperatures today?" Tom complains as sweat pours off his forehead. He wipes his face with a red bandana.

Our Minnesota spring has turned abruptly to summer temperatures. We'd gotten so used to working in chilly conditions, this heat is sucking the energy out of all of us. But Midwest weather is so unpredictable, it could snow tomorrow.

"Let's take a quick break," I say as I hand each of my crewmates a chilled bottle of water.

We settle on the grass beside the partially torn-down building. I spot movement on the Vandervoldts' back patio. An auburn-haired beauty is dragging a lounger out into the sunshine—her striking copper hair shimmers around her shoulders. A tiny Chihuahua runs around at her feet. She's wearing a skimpy bikini and sunglasses. Her curves are on full display as she settles into the chair, ignorant to the fact that she has an audience. This must be the granddaughter. *Gulp.*

Shorty sees her about the same time I do. He whistles under his breath. "I'll gladly review the blueprints with her."

Tom turns to see what the fuss is all about and chokes on the gulp of water he just took, spraying it back out his lips. Coughing for a few seconds, he recovers enough to say, "Dang, I'm going to enjoy this project."

Ignoring them, I finish my water and get back to work. My teammates reluctantly join me while at the same time we all keep a watchful eye on the scantily clad girl in the backyard. Our hammers slam against the old boards, the noise echoing across the yard. We're making quite the racket. The girl shifts around a couple of times on the lounger, glancing pointedly in our direction. *Oh no, are we disturbing the princess?*

Crash! Bang! Bang!

A section of the old exterior wall topples down, the boards landing noisily on top of each other in a messy pile on the uneven ground. We pause, waiting to see what happens next. The occupant of the lounger jumps up, looks at us for a few seconds, then strides towards us. Her dog runs as fast as his little legs will take him in order to keep up. I pull in a sharp breath as I watch her approach. The bikini-clad body is even better when you see it up close.

She stops about ten feet away, puts her hands on her hips and addresses us. "Gentlemen, must you make so much noise? I'm trying to sunbathe over there." She points to the vacated lounger then scoops up the mutt. He glares at us with beady eyes, yipping and acting like a dog twice his size. "Shh Mr. Bean, these men didn't mean to wake you up."

Shorty and Tom look to me for guidance. I guess since I'm a Connor they expect me to take charge of the situation and smooth everything over. I snort under my breath and approach her and the noisy dog. The nice exterior package doesn't fool me. The granddaughter isn't doing anything to dispel my notion that she's just a spoiled rich girl.

"Sorry, miss, but Mr. Vandervoldt asked us to tear down this old building today and that's what we're going to do. You can speak to him if you have issues."

She pushes her sunglasses down her cute nose and glares over them at me. Tom and Shorty stand with their mouths hanging open at my brash response—or maybe it's because of her rocking body. The little dog emits another series of yips, directed right at me.

"I'll address the *noise issue* with Gramps then," she spits each word out, turns on her heel, and stomps back across the lawn with her dog tucked next to her ample chest. She grabs the lounger and drags it, none too gently, back to the patio before disappearing inside. The back door slam acts as an exclamation point to her anger.

I turn back to the job at hand, shaking my head. Tom and Shorty are staring at me.

"Wow, Jacob. I'm surprised you stood up to her. Old man Vandervoldt is probably going to chew us out. Just watch—he'll be out here any minute asking us to quiet down so we don't disturb his granddaughter," Tom says while Shorty nods.

I shrug. "I don't think so. She's being unreasonable. Her grandfather is building the carriage house for her, after all." My words come out a little more vehemently than I expected. This girl doesn't know who she's dealing with if she thinks I'm going to capitulate to her every whim. Even though she rocked that bikini, I'm not going to back down.

Shorty smirks as if he can read my mind.

"Come on, let's get back to work." I motion towards the still half-standing structure. It has stubbornly refused to fall.

Swinging my hammer, I strike a mighty blow to one of the remaining walls. The noise reverberates across the yard. When Tom and Shorty join in, the noise can be heard for miles.

I grin.

11

Chapter Two

Daisy

I take a few calming breaths. Maybe my request for the demolition crew to quiet down was a tad unreasonable. I snicker when I think about the shocked expressions on their faces—all except the guy who stood up to me. He just looked angry. But, man, did he ever appear hunky in his tight, sweaty T-shirt. It hugged all those incredible, manual-labor-developed muscles, obviously not obtained from hours in the gym but from hours swinging a hammer. The sight made my mouth turn dry and my heart rate escalate. Too bad I didn't exactly start off on the best foot with him. His quick dismissal of my complaint was infuriating, and I let my temper get the best of me.

Peeking out the back window, I see that the crew has started working again. The noise is more tolerable in here, so my plans to catch a few rays are cancelled. I confess that the hot temperatures along with the sight of three hunky construction guys tearing down the utility shed lured me outside. And may have influenced my attire. I grin at the desired reaction to my outfit—especially from Mr. Crabby Pants.

"Daisy, there you are." Gramps catches me spying through the window and still wearing my bikini. He raises an eyebrow. "Aren't you a tad underdressed?" His words are belied by his chuckle.

A blush spreads across my cheeks. Holding my towel, book, and sunscreen up to block my scantily clad body, I give my beloved grandfather a sheepish smile. "I met the construction crew. Looks like they're doing a bang up job." *Pun intended.*

He smiles. "Good. I want you to review the final blueprints with one of them today so there aren't any surprises when they start construction tomorrow. Can you do that?"

Nodding, I walk over, kiss him on the cheek, and disappear to my room. I know exactly which member of the crew I'm going to ask to show me those blueprints. My heartbeat accelerates at the thought.

~*~

It takes me several hours to work up the courage to confront crabby guy again. After our little altercation, he probably won't fall all over himself to show me the blueprints like some of the other crew members might. Plus, if he's like most guys, he'll just react to how I look and treat me like a bimbo without a brain. Mr. Crabby Pants is in for a real surprise when he finds out I majored in architecture and that I used to freelance as an architect for smaller construction firms just like Connor Construction. In fact, I've done a few jobs specifically for them in the past. But I doubt they know a female did them because I always sign my work as DM Montgomery. Who'd ever take someone named Daisy Mae Montgomery seriously anyway?

I changed into a more conservative outfit of pink capri pants, a modest white V-neck, strappy sandals, and a jaunty straw hat (to add a bit of fashionista flair and to boost my confidence). Taking a deep breath, I head over to the now-torn-down utility shed while the crew is taking a break. They're sitting on the ground, backs to the yard, discussing something funny. I can hear their laughter as I approach.

Clearing my throat, I address the group. "Grandfather wants me to review the blueprints before you leave."

In unison, the group turns to look at me. They quickly stand and the two lackeys hover behind Mr. Crabby Pants as if he's the one in charge. I raise an eyebrow at him, waiting for him to speak.

"I'd be happy to show you the blueprints. Where would you like to look at them?" The polite reply surprises me after our previous confrontation. His rumbly voice makes shivers run up my neck, and his male magnetism draws me in like I'm a piece of scrap metal from the demolished shed.

For a few beats, I lose my ability to speak. The fine male specimen standing across from me is scrambling my brain. I'm not usually attracted to males who ooze this much testosterone, so I'm caught off guard by my reaction to him. Eventually, I point across the lawn to the patio table. "You can spread the plans out on that table."

He nods and says a few words to his crew, which unfortunately I can't hear. Then he turns back to me. "I'll get the plans from my truck and join you in a few minutes."

My eyes want to stare at his magnificent body for much, much longer, but instead I turn and walk back to the patio.

Settling into one of the cushy patio chairs, I watch as the men collect their tools and load them into their vehicles. They chat for a few minutes, then Mr. Crabby Pants strides over to where I'm sitting while the other two guys flee the scene.

Gulping as the candidate for the cover of *GQ* magazine approaches, I stand, extend my hand, and say, "We haven't been formally introduced. I'm Daisy Montgomery."

He grasps my hand in a firm handshake. I feel the tingle run all the way up my arm. "Jacob Connor."

No wonder he's in charge. He's one of the Connor brothers. The Connors are a well-known family that dates back to when the small town of Connor's Grove was founded. They're second only to the Vandervoldts in prestige and influence. I smile politely while he spreads out the blueprints on the table. Even though Connor Construction didn't use me to draw up these particular blueprints, I know the original plans very well. But Gramps and I made a few changes, so it takes me a few seconds to absorb the modifications.

Jacob takes my staring at the prints as confusion, so he proceeds to explain them to me. He's solicitous in how he explains, and I play along as if I need the help, while at the same time suppressing my laughter. I can't seem to drop the airhead act around him. His muscular forearms draw my attention away from the blueprints. Who knew forearms were so sensual? Gulping, I try to focus back on what he's saying.

Long-winded explanation finished, he pauses. "Do you have any questions?" Jacob looks at me with a pair of mesmerizing sky-blue eyes. His thick brown hair and stubble beard remind me of a hunky firefighter. *Mr. I'll Set Your Heart on Fire March.*

My brain finally sputters back into gear. Returning my eyes back to the plans, I point to the bathroom. "I think this powder room needs a window." My fingers trace along the outer wall, showing him where I'd place it. "The backyard is very private, so we can use a non-frosted window and add a blind if we need to." When I first saw the plans, my instinct was to add that window, so it was my oversight not to add it sooner.

He raises an eyebrow but remains silent.

As I stare at the space that will become the great room, I realize it's going to be too sunny in the late afternoon with all the windows currently called for in the design. That's another change I considered making to the original plans but wasn't quite sure of. Mr. Connor is going to think that I'm one of those clients who constantly ask for revisions. I kick myself for not making these adjustments earlier but I'm not going to apologize for knowing what I want.

"I'm going to use the vaulted great room for painting. While I love the high ceiling and the full wall of windows, the upper ones are going to let in too much sunlight late in the afternoon and can't easily be covered with shades. Remove those, keeping just the lower windows."

This time he nods. "Good point. Any other changes?"

I note a hint of sarcasm in his voice, as if he wanted to add *Your Royal Highness*.

"Not at this time. But I reserve the right to make changes until you hang drywall." Let him chew on that. I look into his eyes, trying to detect his reaction.

He grunts, not committing to that request, but his expression shows his annoyance. I suppress a giggle.

"I'll cover these changes with Max and get updated prints back in a few days . . ." He carefully rolls up the blueprints. "It was a pleasure meeting you, Miss Montgomery."

His voice lacks the enthusiasm expressed by his words. He thinks I'm going to be a troublemaker, wanting change after change of the plans. And why am I playing up the airhead act? I kick myself because it's probably just adding to his low opinion of me.

"Likewise, it was a pleasure meeting you, Mr. Connor." My comment is tinged with sugar and sounds overly saccharine even to my own ears.

Our eyes meet. I see skepticism reflected in his as we exchange handshakes again. He thinks I'm a spoiled bimbo, mooching off my well-to-do grandparents and not working a day in my life. *Darn my outward appearance and my botched first impression.*

Chapter Three

Jacob

Daisy Montgomery is a conundrum. Her suggestions for changes to the carriage house were insightful and spot on. Almost like she knew more about the blueprints than she let on. Maybe she's hiding some brains in that rocking model's body. But, I don't trust the pretty package. Shaking my head, I remember the impractical shoes and the silly straw hat. Who wears that to a construction site?

If today was an example of how this project's going to go, Daisy is trouble. She's the spoiled granddaughter who wants us to bend to her every whim, with no regard to cost or schedule. Let's hope she doesn't cause too much chaos.

Strolling into Connor Construction, I glance at Max's office, but the door is closed. I'm here to discuss the carriage house changes with my brother so we can get them sent off to the blueprint firm as soon as possible. My sister-in-law, the company office manager, is sitting at her desk, looking at the floor. The perplexed expression on her face tells me something's up.

"Hey Hailey, anything wrong?"

She glances up. "I think my water just broke."

My eyes are instantly drawn down to where she's staring, and I notice the puddle under her chair. The sight spurs me into action. "What? Did you call Quinn? Are you having any contractions?" The words spill from my lips in a panic as I pace back and forth.

"I've been having small pains all morning, but I figured it was false labor . . . My due date isn't until next Thursday." She bites her lip. "No, I haven't called Quinn yet."

That statement further escalates my alarm. "Max!" I yell towards the closed door; hopefully my brother is inside.

I kneel beside Hailey not really knowing what to do. "Want me to call Quinn?" Her husband, my oldest brother, is an attorney, known for being calm under pressure. We need his level head and unflappable demeanor at a time like this.

She smiles as my other brother strides from his office. "Jacob, what's up?" His brows draw together when he sees me kneeling beside Hailey and the water on the floor.

"Hailey's water just broke."

"What?" he exclaims. "Did she call Quinn?"

Our sister-in-law giggles as her two strapping brothers-in-law panic over the situation. "Calm down, guys. I'll call Quinn and we'll head to the hospital. I've still probably got hours left." She turns calmly in her chair and dials her cell phone. It rings and rings and she leaves a quick message. Hailey bites her lip again. "He's in court today and isn't answering."

Max and I share a look—somewhere between frustration and fear. *How can our big brother not be available at a time like this?*

"I'll take Hailey to the hospital and you go pull Quinn out of court." Max takes charge and I gladly let him. His wife Maddie is pregnant with twins, so this will be good experience for the dad-to-be.

Collecting her purse from her desk, Hailey stands, then waddles towards the break room. Her stomach protrudes so far from her small frame she looks like she's carrying a beach ball hidden under her voluminous blue dress.

"I'll get some paper towels and clean up the mess," she says over her shoulder.

"No!" both Max and I shout.

"I've got it, Hailey. You go with Max." I gently redirect her towards the front door.

She laughs but follows my order. "Max, can we stop by my house? I need to get my overnight bag." Hailey pauses, putting her hands on her knees. I stand behind her, feeling helpless as she grimaces and breathes rapidly through her nose. *Is she alright? Is this normal? Should we call an ambulance?* After a good half a minute, she stands up again, rubbing her lower back with her hands. "That one was a doozie. Maybe we better get going." She pulls out her phone and swipes her finger across the screen a few times. I figured she's calling Quinn again, but she just looks expectantly up at Max.

With that, Max frantically dials his cell phone. His voice comes out higher than usual. "Sweetie, Hailey's water just broke and she's having contractions." He frowns. "No, I haven't timed them." Hailey grins and taps her phone. *Ah, so that's what she was doing. They have an app for that?* After a few more seconds Max nods. "Yes, she's doing okay but can you meet us at her house? She wants her overnight bag and I want you to stay with her while I go in and get it." He smiles and chuckles. "Love you too," he says, then disconnects.

I smirk at him and he shrugs. "What? She teased me about getting practice for the birth of the twins." When he blushes I conclude that the teasing was too personal for my innocent ears. Maddie and he have been married for five months, but you'd never know they weren't newlyweds. Come to think about it, Hailey and Quinn act the same way. Do Connor men ever get over the honeymoon phase?

Max holds onto Hailey's arm as if she could break, helping her waddle as quickly as possible to the front door. "Maddie is meeting us at your house . . ."

I don't hear the rest of the conversation as they walk out the door.

Placing the forgotten blueprints on Max's desk, I clean up the . . . water, then rush to my car and head to the courthouse to get the unreachable father-to-be.

~*~

The courthouse parking lot is packed. I've tried calling Quinn a few more times in case he got Hailey's message and is already on his way to the hospital. No luck so far. I finally find a spot, park, and jog into the stately limestone building. The security guard, a friend from high school, waves to me as I walk through the metal detector.

From previous experience with a traffic ticket, I know that the courtrooms are all on the second floor, so I run up the stairs. I peer in the first door where what looks like an adoption is taking place. There's balloons and everyone is wearing a T-shirt sporting the phrase "Welcome Dinger to the family." I shake my head at the kid's odd name.

The next door opens to reveal an empty room. I'm starting to worry because there's at least ten rooms on this floor. Will I have to search all of them?

Moving on to door number three, I fling it open and we have a winner. My body sags in relief. Quinn is standing in front of the courtroom with his back to me, talking to a middle-aged man wearing an outdated plaid suit jacket. Just like on TV, the man is sitting in the elevated witness chair to the right of the judge. Quinn is so absorbed in what he's doing, he doesn't notice me as I walk up the aisle. The judge and deputy both frown as I approach the bench.

"What do you want, young man?" The deputy says, getting up from his chair as if he's going to grab his gun and escort me from the room.

My brother turns and his eyes widen. A surprisingly panicky expression crosses his face.

"Quinn, your wife is on her way to the hospital. Her water broke and she's in labor."

Murmurs circulate around the courtroom. A member of opposing counsel stands. "Your honor I propose that we adjourn until tomorrow, or until Quinn becomes a new father." Applause breaks out over the room.

The soon-to-be dad blushes while the judge smiles and whacks her gravel down. "Agreed. Quinn, go join your wife at the hospital. And text me a picture of the new baby."

He turns towards me. "Is anyone with Hailey? She isn't driving herself, is she?" Quinn's words spill out in a breathless rush, telling me he's not holding it together very well.

I put a calming hand on his arm, his panic inspiring me to be the level-headed one right now. "Max and Maddie are with her. I'm sure Mom and Ash will also be on their way."

My brother packs up his legal materials in a rush, stuffing them haphazardly into his bag. The witness on the stand fist pumps the air and shouts, "Way to go, Mr. Quinn."

Laughter follows us as we rush out. Once we're down the stairs and out of the courthouse, I ask, "Are you ready for the new baby?"

Quinn laughs. "She's coming whether her daddy is ready or not." He looks pensive as he gets in his car, then grins up at me. "But I can't wait to meet her."

"I'll join you at the hospital," I shout as he drives out of sight.

Chapter Four

Daisy

Work commenced on the construction project this morning as soon as all the building materials were delivered. But hunky Mr. Connor isn't here. My heart drops in disappointment. Since I'm itching to know why he's absent, I wander out to the construction zone where Luke Anderson introduces himself as the project foreman. The other two workers from the day before wave to me and I wave back.

"Where's Jacob?" I ask as casually as possible. "He and I discussed a few changes to the blueprints yesterday."

Luke nods. "He called me, and I picked up the changes from the office this morning. We should have updated plans by tomorrow."

I frown. I wasn't worried about the blueprints. How do I get him to answer my question about Jacob's whereabouts?

"Jacob's sister-in-law had a new baby." The short guy from the crew shouts the answer to my question from his perch by the chop saw. I smile at him.

Luke turns back to me. "Hailey had her baby, but the little girl made her entrance around two in the morning. The whole family was there, so Jacob's probably sleeping right about now." He peers down at his watch.

"That's wonderful! What's the baby's name? How much did she weigh?" I met Hailey at a community college event one time, and I feel like I know her since she's Jacob's sister-in-law. *Should I send a card?*

The three men exchange baffled looks. It obviously didn't occur to them to ask for these important pieces of baby intel. Luke shrugs, then resumes measuring and sawing wood, giving me a hint that our conversation is over.

I see Gramps sipping coffee on the back patio, so I walk back over to join him. He chuckles and nods towards the construction site when I sit down. "Are they doing things to your satisfaction?"

Smiling, I grab the extra coffee mug and pour some of the hot beverage from the carafe on the table. Gramps and I always share morning coffee, so he came prepared. He slides a plate of Grandma Erma's delicious peach coffee cake towards me. I grab a piece.

After the caffeine enters my system, I finally reply to the question. "We'll know more once they get some of the walls up. They're fast workers, so that's a positive."

He shakes his head, looking thoughtful. "You're in charge, Daisy. If you don't like anything, I know you won't be shy. You'll let them know and get it fixed."

My heart soars at his confidence in me. He's been my anchor since I moved back to Minnesota and got out from under my father's dictatorship. I nod and take a nibble of the moist and tasty cake, thankful to have Gramps in my corner.

~*~

The carriage house is taking shape with almost all the framing complete. A couple rain delays kept me and the crew at bay for a few days, but today is bright and sunny with temperatures in the 80s. Hammering greets me when I settle on the back patio to enjoy my start-of-the-day coffee. Gramps is at the lumberyard this morning, so I'm alone except for Mr. Bean napping at my feet. I can spy on Jacob Connor as much as I want.

He's a sight to behold. His take-charge attitude and muscled frame make me swoon. Too bad I got off on the wrong foot with him. I've got to prove I'm not the spoiled airhead I portrayed that first day. It's time for me to make another appearance at the jobsite under the pretense of making sure my changes to the blueprints were implemented. Truth be told, I just want to interact with Mr. Crabby Pants again. But I need to make my approach carefully.

As I saunter up to the pile of lumber where the men are measuring and sawing, Mr. Bean yips at my feet, getting the crew's attention. Jacob frowns at both me and my dog, but quickly plasters a neutral expression on his face. The other two guys smile pleasantly as if they're happy to see me.

"I don't know your names," I say as I approach the other crew members, ignoring Jacob. Playing a little hard to get never hurts.

The short guy rushes over, shaking my hand vigorously. "I'm Shorty." He scratches my dog's ears, making a friend for life. The brown Chihuahua licks his hand.

"I'm Tom," the other guy says, but he hangs back and waves at me instead of coming over for a handshake.

Still trying to ignore Mr. Connor, who looks delicious in his tight T-shirt, I ask, "Where's foreman Luke?" I stand on my toes, peering over the tall pile of lumber, but I don't see him.

"He's at another job this morning. May I help you?" Jacob replies in a frosty voice. It sounds like I've managed to irritate him again. All part of my plan to get under Mr. Connor's skin. *Behave, Daisy*, a little voice inside my head warns.

If my unconventional childhood taught me anything, it was how to get a man's attention. But I suspect my approach with Jacob isn't having the desired positive effect. I need to regroup, but instead I say, "No, I just wanted to review progress with the man in charge. That's all." I mentally kick myself again as I continue to push Mr. Connor's buttons. I tell myself that his crabby looks and grunts, which I find surprisingly attractive, are inspiring my bad behavior.

He frowns. "You can review progress with me," he spits out, enunciating "review progress" as if it's a dirty word.

"Great," I reply sweetly as I walk towards the framed shell that will eventually be my home. He trails behind me. The rest of the crew hovers in the background. The grass here is a little uneven, making it a bit tricky to navigate.

"Watch your step, wouldn't want you to turn an ankle in those impractical shoes."

I look over my shoulder and glare at his insult. The strappy wedge sandals enhance my legs in the blue jean shorts, and I selected them specifically to catch Mr. Connor's eye. Apparently they did, just not in the way I meant . . .

Ignoring his comment, I stride forward and promptly trip on a board hidden by the tall grass. I teeter on the edge of my elevated shoes, about to unceremoniously face-plant, but Jacob grabs me by the waist to keep me from falling. My hands smack into his solid chest, but he doesn't move a muscle as he steadies me. Our eyes lock for a few seconds. My pulse skyrockets at the casual contact. I reluctantly pull back. Steady again on my feet, I recover from the awkward moment and survey what will eventually be the great room.

Jacob points to the blueprints sprawled across a makeshift worktable of two sawhorses and a piece of plywood. "Did you want to review the updated plans?"

I carefully pick my way to the worktable so as not to trip again. Mr. Connor is correct that these shoes are impractical for the construction zone. Once more, I'm looking like an airhead. I suppress a grimace.

Jacob towers over me as he points to the changes I requested. "We eliminated the upper windows." He then points towards the top of the framed wall. "The lower windows are nine-foot, as called for in the original plan. That's what you still want, right?"

Part of me wants to change them to ten-foot windows, just to be ornery, but I smile serenely and nod in agreement instead. I better behave or I'm never going to change his attitude towards me.

We walk the perimeter of the room, Jacob pointing out windows and doors. They've done a great job with the framing; everything looks square and solid. *Maybe I better double check?*

"May I have a tape measure?" My question catches him off guard. I see the flare of suppressed anger in his eyes as he stomps over to the worktable, returning with a huge tape measure that takes two people to operate. I raise an eyebrow, which he ignores.

Pointing to the far side of the room, I hand him the end of the tape. "Please walk over there, so I can get a measurement."

He rolls his eyes, pulling the tape to where I instructed. I note the measurement, then peer at the blueprints.

"You're off by three millimeters," I say calmly, knowing the miniscule amount is too minor to bicker about. *Why do I keep pushing his buttons?*

He crosses his arms over his sculpted chest. "Miss Montgomery, boards aren't perfect when we get them from the lumberyard. Three millimeters is within normal tolerances."

"I see . . ." I tap my toe as we face off. He drums his fingers on his crossed arms, drawing my eyes to those well-defined pecs. Deciding to change strategy, I say brightly, "Well then, nice job. Looks like you and your crew are working *'within tolerances.'*" I make sure to add air quotes around the last two words.

His lips twitch.

After a few seconds, I give him my man-eater smile, the one that brings most men to their knees. It doesn't seem to faze Jacob at all. *Well, I tried.* Time to end his torture for today. "Thanks for the tour, Mr. Connor. I'll let you get back to work."

I wave to Shorty and Tom as I carefully retrace my steps to the back patio and disappear inside.

Once I'm out of sight, I lean against the doorframe and put a hand to my forehead. "Daisy Montgomery, you need to drop the spoiled brat act." I verbally chide myself. There's something about Jacob Connor that brings out the worst in me. I'm certainly not winning him over at this rate.

Chapter Five

Jacob

We watch Miss Montgomery's retreating form. Those sexy sandals make her legs look even longer, and the tight blue jean shorts sway back and forth with every step. She's one good-looking–but infuriating–woman.

"She has a crush on you," Tom observes. Shorty nods fervently.

I turn to my crewmates. "What, are we still in high school?"

Shrugging, Tom adds, "I'm just saying. A woman doesn't give someone grief like she does you unless she wants to get your attention."

"She's annoying, spoiled, and full of herself," I counter. "That's probably just par for the course for her."

Shorty laughs. "Keep telling yourself that, Jacob."

I grunt in denial of Daisy having any redeeming qualities. "Let's get back to work."

The guys exchange a look, then scatter to perform their jobs.

I'm not falling for Daisy's obvious charms. One burned; twice shy, they say. And I've been burned by the nice packaging before. It's not happening this time.

~*~

We've made a lot of progress today. The main floor is completely framed. Will Miss Montgomery come around again to take measurements of our work? I snicker when I remember her face when I set her straight about working *within tolerances*.

Tomorrow we'll frame the loft bedroom and bath upstairs. This compact house is going to be fantastic when we get it done. The modern design is growing on me more and more.

"Let's call it a day, guys," I say.

Tom and Shorty nod, then collect their tools and start off towards their vehicles.

After tidying up the jobsite, I turn towards my pickup. None other than a smiling Daisy Montgomery is waiting, slouching against my truck. My compadres are nowhere in sight. I guess they fled when they saw her.

She straightens when I approach. My eyes narrow at whatever she has in store for me. *Should I get out a protractor so she can ensure all our angles are precise and to spec?*

Daisy looks at her feet for a few beats, then meets my eyes. "Mr. Connor, I owe you an apology. My behavior this morning was insufferable. You and your crew are doing a terrific job. Please forgive me."

Caught off guard, my mouth hangs open and I stare at her for several seconds longer than is normal. She raises an eyebrow and clears her throat under my scrutiny.

I snap my mouth shut. "Apology accepted," I say in a gruff voice as I start loading my tools in the truck, still trying to make a quick exit. "Call me Jacob," I fling over my shoulder.

Walking into my personal space, she gazes into my eyes. "Your acceptance of my apology didn't sound very convincing, Jacob."

I can't help but chuckle. She's too cute for her own pants and she knows it.

A smile crosses her pretty face. "I'm going fishing. Want to join me? Grandma Erma said we can have a fish fry if I can catch enough." The excitement in her voice is contagious and somewhat surprising. *A girly girl likes to fish?*

For the first time, I notice the fishing pole slung over her shoulder. Mr. Bean peaks out of the bag in her hand, staring at me with his beady eyes. His little black nose twitches back and forth. "I don't have a pole." I blurt out the first thing that comes to mind in the wake of her unexpected invitation.

She thrusts the bag containing the tiny dog towards me along with her pole. "No problem. Gramps has another one in the garage. Wait here while I go get it." She runs out of sight before I can make another excuse not to join her. *How do I let myself get roped into these things?*

I look down at the dog. He stares back at me. After a few minutes, he sticks out his tiny tongue and licks my hand. Shaking my head, I scratch behind his perky ears. The little mutt is growing on me.

"I see you've made friends with Mr. Bean." My fishing companion runs up, carrying the second fishing pole. At least she's wearing a pair of old tennis shoes that are practical and sturdy. She's slightly out of breath, drawing my eyes to her well-endowed chest as it rises and falls. *Gulp.*

"Come on, the fishing pond is this way." Daisy gestures for me to follow and I blindly obey. We start walking down the path, heading further towards the back of the Vandervoldt's property. The scenery feels familiar as we pass through a grove of cottonwood trees. I remember fishing in a nearby county lake a couple times when I was a kid. That must be where we're headed.

"Why did you name him Mr. Bean?" I nod towards the Chihuahua I'm still carrying.

Daisy grins. "He's named after our neighbor when I was a child. Mr. Bean was like a grandfather to me."

Keeping the conversation going seems better than lapsing into awkward silence, so I ask, "Where did you grow up?"

"That's a long story," she replies as she sucks in her lower lip.

I point towards the road stretching out in front of us and winding its way through the trees. "I'd say we have plenty of time since the lake isn't even in sight yet."

She pauses and lets out a loud sigh as if telling the story is a real hardship. I didn't mean to make her feel uncomfortable, but she rambles on before I can change the subject. "My mom was a wild child who clashed with Gramps and Grandma. She balked at her conservative parents and all their 'rules.'" Her air quotes around the word *rules* aren't lost on me. She must not agree with her mom's assessment. "Think of their relationship as if Tom Hanks fathered Miley Cyrus."

My lips quirk into a half grin. That parent-daughter duo would be quite a combination.

"As soon as Mom turned eighteen, she couldn't wait to get away from her family legacy, so she moved to the last place on earth a Vandervoldt would go—Las Vegas. She actually became a Vegas show girl. After a whirlwind romance, she married my dad two months later, and had me when she was nineteen." Daisy abruptly stops walking, scrunching up her face and shaking her head. I halt as well, wondering what's coming next.

"If you knew my dad, you'd be shocked that he ever did an impulsive thing in his life." Our eyes meet and she shrugs, "Whatever." She proceeds on down the path and I join her while she starts back up with the story. "My parents divorced when I was eight months old. Mom stayed in Las Vegas and we lived in a decrepit apartment building where Mr. Bean—the neighbor, not the dog—was the super. He used to watch me when Mom had to perform."

My eyes widen at the briskly told story. A Vandervoldt became a Las Vegas show girl?

I must have vocalized my question without realizing it, because Daisy nods. "Yeah, my mom is definitely what you'd call the black sheep of the family. Gramps and Grandma aren't exactly proud of what she did. Especially the d-i-v-o-r-c-e part," she whispers the spelled-out word behind her hand as if someone is lurking in the woods and can overhear us.

This story was not what I expected. I suddenly need to know more. "Did you always live in Vegas with your mom?"

She hesitates, pausing again in her tracks, then says, "I guess you want to know the whole story, so here goes . . ." She squints her eyes with a reflective look on her face as if she's organizing the story in her head. "Mom and I lived in that tiny, run-down apartment until I was ten. I remember how the ugly shag carpet smelled like spilled milk and the linoleum floors were scuffed and cracked. But it was home to me, especially with Mr. Bean around. He was a navy man and had all sorts of tales to tell. Traveling the world sounded exciting and fun, so when Mom decided to move to Reno, I thought it would be an adventure just like Mr. Bean described."

We start walking again as my companion sucks in her cheeks with a sad expression on her face.

I nudge her long. "The move wasn't fun or exciting, was it?"

Daisy shakes her head. "One move turned into nine moves. We never settled down for very long. I call it the vagabond period of my childhood." Continuing to walk, Daisy adjusts the fishing pole to her other shoulder, then launches back into her tale of woe.

"We lived with Ken in Reno. He was a long-haul truck driver, so we didn't see him very often. Mom got a job at a casino delivering drinks to gamblers, basically a high-class waitress. The tips kept us afloat. When she tired of Ken, we followed a high roller from the casino named Enrique Gomez to Arizona. He was a baseball coach of some sort for the Texas team."

"Texas Rangers?" I feel compelled to ask because my best friend from high school played for them—as if that has anything to do with her story.

Daisy shrugs. "Once spring training ended, Enrique disappeared. We stayed in Phoenix and settled into a cramped room at the Holiday Inn Express where Mom worked the front desk and other odd jobs in exchange for lodging. I'll always remember how the room smelled like greasy fried food because it was right beside the bar. I never got that odor out of my clothes, no matter how many times I washed them." She wrinkles her nose at the memory. It strikes me as rather odd that her olfactory memory is so acute.

Her childhood is nothing like my stable one. I've lived in Connor's Grove, with a brief stint in nearby Minneapolis, all my life. All these boyfriends and locations are giving me a headache. Daisy wasn't kidding when she called it a vagabond childhood. My ears tune back to the story as she plows on.

"Mom's biggest blunder was when she met Rick Rodriquez. He was a smooth talker who told her she should try to make it as an actress. Don't get me wrong, Mom was beautiful, but who breaks into movies at age thirty? Regardless, we followed Rick to Hollywood where he got Mom several auditions. But one audition turned into a thousand auditions with only a small part in a dishwashing soap commercial to show for her efforts."

She shakes her head and looks at her feet for a few ticks. Scuffing her foot, she kicks a stone on the path and it zings into the ditch. The violence of that kick tells me that she isn't feeling as emotionally detached from these childhood memories as she sounds.

Just as abruptly, Daisy launches back into the story. "By the time Mom got her only acting gig, Rick had moved on to a trashy twenty-something sporting a nose ring and tattoos. After that, we found ourselves living in a studio apartment next to a Waffle House where the smell of bacon surrounded us from morning to night." She creases her nose as if conjuring up the fried pork aroma, then she continues, "Fortunately, Mom's commute to work was only across the parking lot." My companion giggles as she points out the only silver lining in this sad story. "Mom waitressed at the pancake

34

joint until she met Frank Smith, whom she promptly married, hoping to keep some stability in our life. By that time, I was a senior in high school. I'd had enough of constantly moving, plus dealing with Mom's boyfriends and now a husband. So as soon as I graduated high school, I left California, determined to find my father."

I'd been wondering about the missing dad in this saga. Even though I'm not sure I want to encourage more of this long-winded story, I blurt out, "Did you find him?"

Daisy grimaces. "Yeah, I knew that he'd moved back to Minneapolis as soon as he divorced my mom. Mom said he thought we were an embarrassment and that's why he couldn't get away fast enough."

My voice raises. "He called you an embarrassment?"

She nods. "Yep. More than once. One time after we reconnected he told me that he was an idiot to marry my mom. A real lapse of judgement on his part." Blowing out a loud breath, she adds, "But, I digress . . ." She looks reflective as she pauses walking and talking for a few seconds, then continues, "Still, when I first looked my father up after I graduated from high school, he seemed pleased to see me. I enrolled in the University of Minnesota and he paid for my first year's tuition."

I have a feeling there's another twist to the story, so I don't interrupt any further. Instead, I speed up our pace hoping to get to our destination before night fall.

A squirrel stirs in the forest, drawing both our attention to the noise of rustling leaves. The tiny creature sounds much bigger than he is as he disturbs our peace and quiet. Once he scampers off, Daisy picks right back up where she left off, "Father kept pushing me to major in what he wanted rather than what I wanted. Business administration was a real bore." She rolls her eyes. "I wanted to major in a more creative field. He put his foot down, so I agreed, but I flunked out sophomore year. That's when I looked up my grandparents. When I was a child, we never saw Gramps or Grandma because Mom wasn't speaking to them. But I was desperate and in need of financial assistance, so my reason for looking up my grandparents was purely mercenary at the time."

My eyes widen at her blunt honesty. She hasn't had a typical Vandervoldt upbringing. And she isn't afraid to admit that the Vandervoldt's bank account was what initially drew her to them.

"My grandparents immediately offered to pay for my tuition, room, and board. I could major in anything I wanted to. Reaching out to my grandparents was the best decision I ever made. When I graduated from U of M, Gramps encouraged me to come live with them; that's when he came up with the plan to build the carriage house for me. So, here I am." She shrugs her shoulders as if there's nothing uncommon in the story she just recounted.

Daisy's sad tale is helping me see her in a different, more sympathetic, light. "How about your mom? Does she still live in California?"

"Yep, she's on her fifth marriage." Stopping, she turns to me, "I certainly don't have any good role models for marriage or happily ever after. Except for Gramps and Grandma Erma. They'll be married fifty years this June." Reaching over to scratch Mr. Bean's head, she adds, "When I was a child, I thought I was unlovable since Mom basically ignored me and I never saw my father. Then I met Mr. Bean. He was my savior."

Her story comes full circle to my original question. A tear rolls down her cheek, but she quickly swipes it off with her thumb. She squints directly at me. "I don't know why I'm telling you all this."

I'd wondered the same thing, but maybe with our volatile start, Daisy wanted to show me another side of her.

As if she needs space between her soul-baring confession and me, Daisy strides off. I stand flat-footed for several minutes, giving her some time and space. Mr. Bean yips from the bag in my hand. When he tries to scramble out, I run to catch up to his pretty master.

We walk in companionable silence as I digest what she told me. I don't know of a single Connor who's been divorced. As my mom would say, "The Connors stick it out through thick and thin." Although she may have been referring to the Thanksgiving Day blizzard of 1896 that my great-grandparents survived.

The trees thin out and we're greeted by a small lake surrounded by a sandy, rocky shoreline. The blue water sparkles as the afternoon sun hits it at just the right angle. When we find a level spot on the shore, we stand several feet apart so our lines won't tangle. I break the silence that's fallen between us. "I'm glad you found your Gramps and Grandma." My opinion of her has changed drastically. She's not a spoiled rich girl. Or, at least, she hasn't been for very long.

She beams. "Me too. I love them very much." Mr. Bean hops out of his bag and sits beside her.

After a few minutes, I look out of the corner of my eye, and Daisy is trying to bait her hook. I smirk to myself, just waiting for her to beg me to deal with the slimy bait. *Worms are icky,* I predict she'll say.

She's biting her lip in a look of complete concentration as she carefully puts the night crawler on the hook. I get a little squeamish myself watching her squish the worm into position. Once she has the hook baited to her satisfaction, she pulls back her rod and makes a skillful cast. The bobber plops about twenty feet out in the lake. She sits down on a flat rock, then grins over at me.

Shock and humor must be apparent on my grinning face.

"What?" she asks.

"I'm just surprised. That's all." Getting my hook ready, I cast out, but my effort is not nearly as far into the lake as hers.

She giggles. "What are you surprised about?"

I glance over, her chocolate brown eyes meeting my blue ones. "That you bait your own hook and can outcast me." I want to add "your unconventional childhood" to the things that surprise me about her, but I keep that thought to myself.

We both look out at our bobbers and laugh.

Chapter Six

Daisy

The fishing expedition was a success, not only in the amount of fish we caught, but also in my attempt to repair Jacob's perception of me. Once I started telling my story, I couldn't stop. It was like I had diarrhea of the mouth. He had formed such a poor opinion I guess my inner psyche needed to correct his first impression.

After I told Jacob the dreadful story about my childhood, he warmed up considerably. I didn't push any of his buttons and we got along the whole time. My restraint surprised even me.

Even though he didn't accept my invitation to Grandma's fish fry, I got the vibe that he did have another obligation and that he wasn't making up an excuse. Does he have a girlfriend? Jealousy raises its ugly head in the pit of my stomach at that thought.

Beep beep beep!

Peering out the back window towards the construction site, I see a bulky truck backing up. Vandervoldt Lumber is splashed across the side; a new set of building materials has arrived.

The crew isn't around today—a stoppage due to lack of supplies. I'm currently suffering from Jacob withdrawal, moping at the kitchen island. My favorite pastime at present is spying on or teasing Mr. Connor, and he hasn't been here for two days. My one consolation is imagining the completion of my beautiful new home.

The layout is perfect, and I can't wait to occupy the space. Gramps and I created the design from a plan we found in one of Grandma Erma's *Southern Living* magazines. Contemporary Carriage House is the name of the layout, and the article touted the plan as "a charmingly comfortable, compact guest space with modern touches." In the original plan, the first floor was an area to park vehicles (thus the carriage house moniker); we converted it to a great room and kitchen. The upstairs is a cozy bedroom and bath. It's tiny but just what I need.

Lately, I've become bored with architecture because everyone builds the same floor plan over and over. This turned my little architecture firm into a rote business where I just recycled the same plan from customer to customer. No one in this small town wants to vary too much from the norm. Only Gramps is brave enough and visionary enough to build something unique. And my little carriage house is definitely unique.

Although I have a double major in architecture and graphic design, I haven't focused on trying to build a graphic design business. But I want to. I also paint and have sold several paintings at local art fairs. My new career goal is to focus on my artwork and graphic design rather than my architecture. Gramps has been so supportive of my goals. But, my father not so much. He said, and I quote, "Why do you want to do that artsy-fartsy stuff when architecture pays the bills? Stick with what works."

Truthfully, I'm not very good at sticking to anything for very long. Fresh out of college I worked at an architecture firm in Minneapolis, but I got tired of the big city. When I moved in with my grandparents I started my architecture firm, got bored with that, and then dabbled in personal photography, taking family portraits and documenting weddings. After a few months, I hated the long hours and dealing with the bridezillas. Last winter I interned at a Saint Paul advertising agency and loved it. They even allowed me to work remotely. Unfortunately, that gig ended when they decided not to extend the internship to a permanent position due to budget constraints.

Sighing, I face the reality that I flit from one career to the next. When I get bored or frustrated, I move on. Guess I take after Mom.

A floral scent alerts me that my sweet grandmother is about to join me in the kitchen. "Daisy Mae, what are you so glum about?"

"Nothing," I mumble.

She smiles. "You're missing that nice young man, aren't you?" Her eyes swivel towards the empty construction site.

"Maybe," I reply as a blush spreads across my cheeks.

"I always say the best way to a man's heart is through his stomach. How about you make him a tasty dessert. What do you think he'd like?"

I perk up. Grandma always knows how to cheer me up. "Can we make your famous German chocolate cake?" My mouth waters at the thought.

"Let me find the recipe."

~*~

Pounding wakens me, and I fling off my covers, running over to the window. Unlike the first day of construction, I'm not complaining about the noise—in fact it's music to my ears. The crew got an early start and Mr. Connor is here wearing a tight black T-shirt and khaki shorts. I lick my lips.

Saving the German chocolate cake surprise for lunch, I waltz out to the back patio, positioning myself so I can watch the crew (okay I really mean so I can watch Jacob) without being obvious. I stretch out in the lounger, open my romance novel, and start to read. Mr. Bean naps at my feet. After re-reading the same paragraph about the duke's chiseled chest four times, I give up and just watch the construction action over the top of my book. Real-life Jacob is much yummier than the fictional duke.

The men are shingling the roof, lifting heavy packs of shingles and using nail guns to tack them into position. Jacob working is a sight to behold. As the temperatures climb, the guys shed their shirts. Sweat glistens off their bodies, showing off every muscle and contour. I'm hot in my shorts and T-shirt just sitting here—and possibly also from the sight of a certain sexy man. I fan my face.

About an hour in, the crew takes a break, gulping down bottled water, laughing, and chatting. Mr. Bean's ears perk up at the noise. He hops down from the lounger and tears across the backyard towards the men. I squeak and run after him, shouting and waving at them. I don't want them to crush my little dog if they don't see him. My cute but impractical wedge sandals once again slow my progress.

Jacob spots the Chihuahua before I get very far. He scoops him up as Mr. Bean wiggles his whole body in joy. He licks Jacob's face, making him laugh. *Mr. Bean has a crush on Mr. Connor too.*

I slow up as Jacob approaches me with the small dog. It's a funny sight to see the big, muscular guy gently carrying such a tiny animal. I grin.

He stops a few steps from me. "Did you lose something?" he asks with a smirk.

I close the distance between us, petting Mr. Bean's head. "You naughty boy," I say, but my voice doesn't sound very much like a scolding.

Jacob reaches up to pet the dog's head at the same time. His naked, sweat-glistening chest is inches from my hands. Time stands still. His male charisma makes me feel light-headed. I pause petting the dog while we gaze at each other for several seconds. I see attraction in Jacob's eyes, and he doesn't look like he's fighting it. Neither am I.

A noise from the construction site interrupts our moment. Jacob smiles, handing me the errant dog. "He's just a little squirt and I wouldn't want anything to happen to him."

My susceptible heart goes pitter patter—this man's appeal grows by leaps and bounds. It's so sexy when a guy shows his soft side.

When he starts to turn around, I add in a shy voice, "Mr. Connor, would you like to have lunch with me on the patio?" My heart is beating out of my chest and my fingers are crossed, hoping that he doesn't reject my offer.

A slow smile lights up his face. "I accept your lunch invitation, Miss Montgomery." He strides off while I admire the view. He beats the chiseled-chest duke hands down.

Chapter Seven

Jacob

She's getting under my skin. The Daisy I went fishing with was sweet and friendly. We had absolutely the best time. After our rocky start, I didn't see myself wanting to have anything to do with her. Now I've agreed to have lunch with her. I shake my head in disbelief.

When noontime rolls around, I see her setting out food on the patio. How is this going to look to my crewmates? I jump in, getting the awkward situation over with. "I'm having lunch with Miss Montgomery."

With that announcement, Tom and Shorty drop the pack of shingles they were picking up back on the ground. After a few beats, Tom says, "Well that seals it, we're going to Snappy Stop to get hamburgers. You enjoy your lunch with *Miss Montgomery.*"

"I told you she has a crush on you," Shorty adds. He elbows Tom and they snicker. Both wiggle their eyebrows at me as they walk away.

My mouth hangs open at how easily they let me off the hook. More teasing is coming later, I'm sure.

The lush grass rustles under my feet as I approach the patio. Daisy turns and smiles at me. My breath catches at her beauty. She's wearing the hip-hugging pink capri pants again and a white t-shirt that clings to all her curves. Those impractical sandals are once again strapped to her feet. I want to pull her into a hug and kiss her until she's breathless. Instead, I take in the scrumptious food spread out on the round table.

"I hope sandwiches are okay. Grandma also made potato salad." She twirls the ring on her pinky finger, looking apologetic for some reason.

"This looks delicious," I say, hoping to steady her nerves and break the awkwardness suddenly surrounding us.

She smiles shyly up at me. "Oh good. Sit down and let's eat." Daisy motions to the chair across from her.

I smile and plant my butt in the chair, then she joins me. We build our sandwiches in silence, passing bread, turkey, Swiss cheese, and condiments back and forth between us. Daisy grabs a handful of chips, then passes me the bag. I add a big lump of potato salad to my plate—it's my favorite.

Daisy gestures at an open cooler with a wide variety of drinks inside. "Would you like a cold soda? I didn't know what you like, so I brought out a selection."

I smile at her thoughtfulness and select a can of Dr. Pepper.

"That's my favorite too," she says as she takes the other Dr. Pepper sitting in the cooler. The can fizzes loudly when she pops the top. She takes a sip and then wiggles her nose when the carbonated beverage teases it.

Mr. Bean sits at Daisy's feet, swiveling his tiny head back and forth as he watches us eat. He's on high alert for any dropped crumbs. I sneak him a small piece of turkey.

"You're spoiling him."

I shrug. "Us guys have to stick together."

She laughs, then asks, "Have you always worked for Connor Construction?"

I should have expected this question. I glance down at my plate and pretend to focus on taking a bite of my sandwich. "No. I used to work at an advertising agency in Minneapolis. They laid me off last year." A frown crosses my face at the mention of my shattered career aspirations. I put my heart and soul into that job, sacrificing family get-togethers and personal pursuits to work overtime at a company that didn't appreciate me whatsoever. They strung me along, dangling the carrot of future promotions when all they wanted was more effort. Shrugging, I add, "The timing was good because my brother Max got hurt, so I took his position on the construction team. He owns and operates the company."

Daisy perks up. "I worked as an intern at an ad agency in Saint Paul, but they didn't extend my position due to 'budget constraints.'"

I nod knowingly. Ad agencies are such tightwads.

"I'd like to get back into graphic design. Gramps is encouraging me to start my own company."

I pause eating my sandwich. "Really? When I first came back to Connor's Grove, I thought I'd try to start an ad agency, but I kind of got sidetracked with the construction gig."

My lunch companion leans forward and her smile broadens. "If I didn't think we would kill each other, we could start something together."

Chuckling, I nod, pondering how that could work. Are we too much like Mr. Darcy and Elizabeth Bennet? Having that analogy pop into my head surprises me because I slaved over reading that Jane Austen tome in high school.

Daisy focuses my wandering thoughts. "Actually, I'm serious. I have two friends with backgrounds in advertising and marketing. They're both between gigs and available."

Her proposition rattles around in my brain for a bit. "Can we get your friends together to discuss this? I don't want to abandon the construction crew just yet since Max's wife Maddie is having twins in a few months. But I'd commit half my time to a new venture."

Daisy squeals. "Twins! I've always wanted to have twins."

I raise my eyebrow at the abrupt change of topic. "Talk to Maddie after a few months and see if you change your tune."

"Ha. Ha. Very funny," she replies and swats me in the arm as she collects our empty plates. "I'll be right back with dessert." She winks and disappears through the French doors with her butt swaying back and forth. Daisy is a delectable dessert herself.

Miss Montgomery returns carrying a large cake dripping with coconut icing. "My grandma's German chocolate cake," she announces, then plops the plate in the middle of the table.

Ah, Erma's famous German chocolate cake. I've heard all about it from Quinn and Hailey. Erma even baked them one for their wedding.

Daisy cuts me a thick slice. I savor the gooey goodness as it slides down my throat. "This is delicious. You made this?"

She blushes. "Yep. It took me three hours yesterday. You have to wait until the cake is completely cool in order to ice it."

"It was worth all your time." I almost lick the plate in order to get every crumb.

She smiles. "When can you get together to talk about our new business venture?" I thought maybe she had conveniently forgot about this topic when she enthused over the twins.

Getting out my phone, I consult my calendar. Between Mom and Ash, I'm booked with family events, one of them being the baby arrival party for Quinn and Hailey. Of course, the Connors (namely Mom) take every opportunity to celebrate, despite the fact we already had a baby shower for the happy couple.

"Looks like I'm open in two weeks. How about Wednesday night?"

She nods. "I'll call Ford and Sylvie and let you know whether that works." Looking at my empty plate, she adds, "Do you want another slice of cake?"

Knowing I'll burn off the calories installing shingles this afternoon, I grin. "Yes, please."

Chapter Eight

Daisy

Since work started on the carriage house two months ago, the construction has progressed well. Framing is done and the shell is enclosed. The interior finishing is just starting to take shape with drywall complete and the kitchen ready for cabinets and tile. I'm excited to see everything come to together and my vision become a reality.

After my lunch with Jacob, I've played nice, and not one time did I insist on measuring anything. Now that they're starting on the interior, I want to get more hands on, which will mean more interactions with Jacob. Maybe I shouldn't push his buttons anymore? *Naw, what fun would that be?*

When I arrive at the house this morning, only Shorty is there. He's staring at the kitchen wall, then glances down at his watch when I walk in. Apparently Jacob's been sent to another jobsite to help for a few hours and Tom is under the weather.

Even though he's the same height as me, Shorty is cute in his own way. His curly brown hair always looks mussed, with a couple curls tumbling onto his forehead. He's charmingly polite and has never been crabby in my presence (unlike another member of the team I won't mention). But I don't feel any attraction towards him at all. *Funny how chemistry works.*

"Miss Montgomery, are you up to helping me with the backsplash tile in the kitchen?" Shorty asks. "It would go a lot faster with an extra pair of hands."

Since I've always wanted to learn how to install tile, I reply enthusiastically, "I'm in."

He laughs.

We open boxes of tile and arrange them on a piece of plywood lying on the island across from where we'll be doing the installation. The tiles come in six-inch-by-twelve-inch sheets. The pattern is a mix of glass rectangles in five different shades of gray, with small, medium, and large rectangles making up each sheet.

I peer at the small print directions on the side of the box and read them aloud, "It's recommended that you open several boxes and mix sheets from different cartons in order to get a pleasing, more random mixture. The manufacturer does not guarantee a random mix of sheets within a carton."

My coworker snorts.

"What?" I ask.

"They just want you to open all the cartons so you can't take them back to the store."

I laugh.

Shorty keeps me amused as we have fun moving sheets around, trying different combinations of the tile pattern. We work for the better part of the morning unloading boxes and sliding the sheets on our work surface until we get the pattern I like. I'm sure if I had done this little exercise with Mr. Connor, we'd still be debating how to arrange the first two sheets. On the other hand, Shorty follows my directions without argument.

"Miss Daisy, why couldn't you choose white subway tile? It's much easier to work with—all one color and size," my disgruntled coworker says as he points to our sorting effort. "We had to work two and a half hours to achieve this pleasing, random pattern." He smirks. "And we had to open all nineteen boxes."

I'm giggling at his hilarious remark when Jacob strides in. The Mr. Crabby Pants scowl is back on his handsome face. *Is he jealous of Shorty and me working together?*

"Morning, Jacob," Shorty says, apparently oblivious to the vibe Jacob is emitting in my direction. "Luke wants you to start putting down the hardwood floor in the great room. We're down a man since Tom is out sick. Daisy's been helping me so I can get the tile

49

done today, because the kitchen countertops are coming tomorrow."

I give Jacob a flirty smile which does nothing to dent the scowl on his face.

"Okay, I'll start on the floor," Mr. Crabby Pants says in a gruff voice as he looks at the tile spread out on the island. I could listen to that sexy voice all day because it makes tingles run up my spine.

Jacob disappears and soon after I hear: *Bam!* silence, *Bam!* repeatedly coming from the great room.

"Sounds like he's working off a little excess energy," Shorty says with a chuckle. He winks at me and I blush. Shorty isn't as clueless as he lets on.

We develop a sort-of working rapport. Shorty and me working in the kitchen and Jacob slamming and nailing wood flooring into place in the great room.

Once the tile pattern is all laid out and ready to go, Shorty shows me the next step. "Apply the mortar in a swirl pattern on the wall," he says as he demonstrates. He drags some of the thick mortar onto his trowel and smooths it on the wall, making it look easy.

"May I try it?"

Shorty nods, so I take the trowel from him. My first attempt is clumsy and looks nothing like what he did. I laugh at my awkwardness. My second attempt is only marginally better.

"We don't have much time to place the tile before the mortar hardens," Shorty mentions casually.

We both snicker as we stare at my mortar, which looks like a two-year-old did it.

"Okay, maybe you better do the mortar then."

After a few minutes, we settle into a good rhythm, with Shorty applying mortar and placing the tile while I hand him the sheets in the pattern we laid out on the island.

Every now and then I stand back to admire our work while spying on what's going on in the great room. Jacob is working at a relentless pace and half the floor is down. It's a beautiful sight—both the hunky guy and the new floor. He's dripping with sweat and I wonder how he can keep that pace going for very long.

Unfortunately I have to turn my full attention back to my task when we get to the tile going in over the cooktop. It's a different pattern than the regular backsplash, more intricate and with varied colors, shapes, and sizes of tile. Our progress goes much slower when we get to this section.

I'm concentrating so much on the tile, I barely notice that the noise from the great room has ceased. Peeking again around the corner, I see Jacob sitting on one of the unopened bundles of wood, admiring his work and drinking a bottle of water. His back is to me and his biceps flex as he takes a swig of water. *Gulp.*

An idea hits me, and I grin.

Returning to assist Shorty, I can't help but take advantage of the silence coming from the other room. I elbow Shorty and whisper to him, "Play along with me, okay?"

He gives me a confused look, then shrugs and turns back to the backsplash.

This time when I hand him a tile sheet, I say in a loud, breathless-sounding voice, "Aaah, you almost have it."

Shorty grins and shakes his head. He now sees where this is going.

"Just a little further to the left. A little further." I wink and almost giggle at the expression on my coworker's face, but I compose myself and keep going. "Oooh, yes. Right there. Yes! Yes! Yes!"

Shorty's eyes widen further as the words tumble from my mouth. The rapture in my voice sounds like Meg Ryan in *When Sally Met Harry*. My performance is almost Oscar worthy.

On cue, Jacob strides into the kitchen, his boots pounding on the floor as he approaches.

I put on my best angelic face as I turn to look at Mr. Crabby Pants while Shorty places the sheet of tile on the wall. My companion's shoulders shake with laughter, and I hope he doesn't give us away.

"What's going on in here?" Jacob says in a none too friendly voice. He stands with his hands on his hips and glares at us. I bite my tongue in order to suppress a giggle.

"I was directing Shorty how to position the tile on the wall," I reply in an innocent voice. "Isn't he doing a great job?" I point to the wall behind me.

Jacob snorts. "Can you keep it down a little?" He turns on his heel and stomps back into the great room where the slamming noise resumes, this time louder and even faster than before. I'd hate to be the wood flooring right now.

Shorty smiles at me and says under his breath, "I think you got his attention. Well played, Miss Montgomery." We high-five.

Chapter Nine

Jacob

A week later and Tom is still under the weather. Did he go camping or fishing under the guise of sickness? Summer is in full swing, so I understand the temptation.

Miss Montgomery may think that she got the last laugh on the tile prank. At the time, I reacted to the situation, unwittingly playing right into her hands. But my plan for payback is brilliant and she'll never suspect a thing until it's too late.

When Daisy arrives, I snag her before Shorty can dream up another project for her to help him with. "Can you help me paint the waterproof barrier on the shower walls? It needs twenty-four hours to dry before we can install the tile. With Tom still out, I need help."

She smiles. "Sure, just show me what to do." Her enthusiasm gives me a little twinge of guilt.

I motion for her to lead the way to the bathroom, which is located upstairs next to the master bedroom. Her perfect derriere sashays as she climbs the stairs. The swaying blue jean shorts capture my attention with how tightly they mold to her hips. The temperature in the room rises ten degrees.

Shorty catches my eye right as I'm turning to follow Miss Montgomery. "You know that stuff smells like sh—"

I cut him off, shaking my head and giving him a firm look.

"Is the paint already upstairs?" I say loudly to cover up Shorty's comment.

He rolls his eyes. "Yep."

From previous experience, I know that the waterproof barrier substance smells worse than a manure pile on a 90-degree day. The smell will be even more pungent in the close confides of the small bathroom. *Oh darn.*

Shaking up the paint can, I find the appropriate bristle brush and show Daisy what to do without opening the paint lid just yet. No need to let the aroma loose in the room any sooner than necessary.

"Apply the paint generously to the wall. Make sure you cover every inch thoroughly. Take long strokes because this stuff is pretty thick." I demonstrate with the dry brush.

Daisy rolls her eyes at my rudimentary explanation. I suppress a laugh.

"I'll be over here working on the cabinets." I point to the far end of the bathroom where I'll be installing the small vanity and overhead cabinets. I pop the lid off the can then retreat to watch the action.

Miss Montgomery loads up her brush liberally and starts applying the thick substance to the shower walls. The paint goes on thick, gooey, and brown, resembling the substance it smells like. After a few strokes, she wrinkles her nose. The horrible odor drifts my way, but I focus on the cabinets as if nothing is amiss.

Daisy keeps painting and the stench keeps building until the odor is almost unbearable. She holds her hand over her nose, makes a gagging noise, but keeps going. I almost feel sorry for her.

About five minutes into the job, Daisy emerges from the shower stall, taking a few deep breaths.

"Is this stuff supposed to be this smelly?" Her voice cracks and she covers her mouth.

"Want me to open the window?" I reply innocently.

She nods vigorously, then returns to her task.

I open the one window in the bathroom but there isn't any breeze, so there's no airflow either. Some of the smell might escape, but without a fan it isn't going to make much of a dent on the pungent odor. My eyes start to water. How can Daisy keep going? I never expected her to last more than two minutes on this task. *Should I tell her to quit? Or offer her a face covering?*

Once she's finished one wall, she walks to the window and breathes deeply. Her nose is red, and her eyes are watering. She swipes moisture from the corners of her eyes with her sleeve.

I never dreamed she would be such a trouper. My admiration for her grows exponentially. After the brief break, she soldiers on. Bending, she tries to load up the brush again. Because the can is getting low, she picks it up and scrapes the bottom. Her nose is only inches away from the can. *That can't be good.*

Daisy stops abruptly, making another, louder gagging sound in her throat.

Bang!

The can hits the floor. She rushes from the bathroom, down the stairs, out the front door, and into the yard. Since she stops right under the bathroom window, I can hear everything clearly. The sounds she's making indicate she's lost her breakfast. All of it. The noise goes on for several agonizing seconds.

At this point, I'm feeling very guilty and sorry for her. I'll go down and tell her she doesn't have to finish the task. Just as I'm laying my tools down, Daisy shuffles back into the bathroom. Her face is pale and she's still looking a little green.

"If you're not feeling well, call it a day. I'll finish painting." I offer up an understanding smile and speak in a conciliatory tone to help overcome my regret over the prank.

She glares at me, then grabs the red bandana hanging from my back pocket. Tying the scarf over her nose, she picks up the paint can and brush, marches back into the shower stall, and continues as if nothing happened.

After we work in silence for several minutes, my guilt weighs heavily on me and I say, "The smell is pretty bad. Go ahead and quit if you need to."

Turning towards me, Daisy puts her hands on her hips. "My stomach's empty now. Why should I quit?"

My lips twitch, but I successfully suppress my laughter.

"Open more paint." She points to the extra cans sitting beside me.

I sigh and shake my head. She's stubborn, infuriating, and I can't resist her.

Chapter Ten

Daisy

I had to wash my clothes three times before that horrible paint smell came out. For days I thought I could detect the manure-like odor in the air—I have what's called hyperosmia, an extreme olfactory sensitivity. Odors, especially unpleasant ones, stick with me forever.

As payback after the painting incident, a few days later I replaced sugar with salt at the Keurig coffee station Grandma kindly setup for the crew. Jacob was the first one at the jobsite that morning, so I pretended to be inspecting the tile backsplash while I watched him put several teaspoons of "sweetener" into his coffee and take a sip.

"Ahh, that's awful!" He said as he spat out the horrible taste. Glaring over at me, he grabbed a water bottle and chugged it.

Neither of us spoke of the switcheroo, but he paid me back later that week when he painted a wall in the master bedroom with neon-pink glitter paint. My eyes hurt just looking at it.

"What is this?" I said after hauling his butt upstairs to show him his handiwork.

"I was just following the instructions on the blueprints," he said with a huff and a half smirk.

Marching back downstairs I opened the prints a bit more forcefully than necessary. Squinting I read the handwritten note with an arrow pointing to the mutilated wall, "Benjamin Moore Posh Pink Glitter. 2 Coats."

Turning back to a smug-looking Jacob, I said, "I didn't approve this."

Leaning closer to the plans and, in the process, imposing on my personal space, Mr. Connor feigned surprise. "You're right, that change wasn't initialed . . . My mistake."

Hands on hips, I replied, "I expect that wall to be back to the approved neutral tone by tomorrow."

"Ah, you mean Manchester Tan?" He coughed "blah" into his hand.

I groaned and stalked away, but the wall was restored to the blah tan the next morning.

Since we can't quit trying to one up each other, I'm being the mature one and calling a truce. If we're going to start an advertising company, we can't keep pushing each other's buttons like two teenagers. Jacob and I are too competitive, and each prank gets more outlandish.

I meet Jacob and Shorty at the carriage house a few days later with a peace offering in hand. "Good morning, gentlemen."

Both men look at me with caution in their eyes. Although Shorty has never been a victim of my stunts, he still looks wary. They grunt in response to my pleasant greeting.

"A peace offering." I place the plate of only slightly burned brownies on the kitchen island. In my defense, I lost track of time and didn't hear the timer go off. Grandma usually saves me from overcooking stuff, but she wasn't around. In the end, the only brownies I had to discard were the charred ones at the edge of the pan. I consider it a win.

The men are installing the rest of the kitchen cabinets. Tools and parts are scattered everywhere. A few upper cabinets hang on the wall and I can tell the cherry finish is going to look incredible in the small space.

I turn to Jacob. "No more shenanigans from you either. My clothes still smell like that horrible paint." I add for dramatic effect, laying on the guilt-trip.

His eyebrows pull together in a grimace. "You eat one first," Jacob says as he waves his hand towards the plate.

Internally rolling my eyes at his slightly unjustified trust issues, I waltz over to the plate, carefully select a brownie and take a big bite. "Umm, yummy," I say.

Neither one of the men makes a move towards the delicious dessert.

"What are you afraid of?"

"You put laxatives in them," Mr. Connor bluntly replies.

My eyes widen. "Would I eat one if that was the case?"

Shorty laughs. Jacobs smirks.

"I'll stay here the rest of the morning just to prove to you that there's nothing harmful in the brownies . . . But I refuse to apply any. . . paint." I point a finger at Jacob.

He looks uncomfortable at my remark. Maybe Jacob does regret the stunt he pulled. "Okay, truce." Jacob says, then shakes my hand. My arm tingles at his touch.

I look over at Shorty. "Well?"

He throws up his hands. "I'm a neutral third party. Like Switzerland."

Both Jacob and I snort.

"We can use your help unpacking all the parts for these cabinets." Jacob hands me three boxes. "Sort them by type into these containers."

"Yes, sir." I salute.

He rolls his eyes. The brownies sit dejectedly on the island.

By lunch, the guys are making good progress on the cabinets. I've sorted all the screws, bolts, nuts, hinges, and other hardware as instructed. I even cleaned up the work area and collected any spare parts into orderly piles.

Truth be told, I love watching Jacob work. Installing the heavy cabinets requires all those splendid muscles to flex and strain under his tight T-shirt. Several times I had to remind myself to breathe.

We work well together, and the men's frostiness is thawing. They tease me and I tease them back. We're all laughing when Luke walks in.

"Looks like you're making good headway." The foreman eyes the space appreciatively. "Will the cabinets be done today?"

Luke's all business, so Jacob and Shorty transform into all business as well. "Yes, we'll have them all installed before we leave," Jacob replies.

Nodding, Luke turns to me. "Miss Montgomery, are you satisfied with everything so far?"

I smile broadly. "Yes, the house is turning out even better than I imagined."

He smiles and checks a clipboard in his hand. "Jacob, I need you tomorrow at the Ferguson site. Shorty, you'll work here."

"Sounds good," Jacob replies.

"Yes, sir," Shorty replies.

"I won't bother you any further. Keep up the good work." He snags a brownie and saunters off.

My palms sweat. Luke just took the one tainted brownie. Bad timing to eat that and then be on the road. I pray he can find a fast food place with a clean restroom when the need arises.

The guys exchange a worried look. *There goes that prank . . . Time to make the best of it.* Putting my hands on my hips, I feign outrage. "There's nothing in the brownies to be concerned about. I haven't had any reaction, have I?"

Both men shrug, then grab a bottled water and a brownie. Jacob sniffs his as if he's an illegal substance detection dog. I nod sweetly encouraging both men to enjoy the treat. When they snarf down the chocolate confection and then take several more, I'm relieved that Luke already cleared out the tainted dessert thus keeping up my ruse. *Maybe I should let this be an actual peace offering and really stop with the pranks.*

60

My satisfaction at their enjoyment of the brownies (and the save by Luke) is short lived as I remember that Jacob has been assigned to a different jobsite tomorrow. With the carriage house nearing completion, I won't see him every day. I need to get the new advertising company kicked off as soon as possible.

Chapter Eleven

Jacob

I haven't seen Daisy for two weeks since I've been reassigned to the Ferguson build. She reminds me of a whirlwind—she comes in, blows things around, and leaves a path of destruction behind her. Lately her destruction has been mostly to my concentration.

"Jacob, can I get you more scrambled eggs?" Mom asks as I stare off into space, thinking about Miss Montgomery.

Without the construction job I'd be gaining weight eating all of Mom's fabulous cooking. I need to look for an apartment and quit sponging off Mom and Dad. Looks like I'll be staying in Connor's Grove for a while. A petite spitfire with a big attitude is strongly influencing that decision.

"No, thanks. I'm full." I glance at the clock on the kitchen wall. "I need to get going."

Mom smiles sweetly at me over her coffee mug. Oh no, I know that look.

"I was talking to Delores yesterday, and her daughter Alicia is in town for the weekend. Why don't you ask her out?" Mom says, then barrels ahead without giving me a chance to speak. "Alicia graduated from Stanford and she's looking for a job in the Twin Cities, so she'll be local. You two have a lot in common."

Putting my arms over my chest, I frown. The only thing we have in common is two meddlesome mothers. "Mom, we've had this conversation a hundred times. I'm not interested in dating right now." Daisy's pretty face pops into my mind.

Taking another sip of her coffee, Mom tries to make me feel guilty with her sad eyes and slumped shoulders. "I just want you to be happy."

I walk over to her and give her a hug. "Mom, I am happy. Working for Connor Construction is a good change of pace."

"I'm so glad to hear that you plan on being in Connor's Grove long term. All my kids are now within a ten-mile radius."

Her interpretation of my last words isn't totally accurate, but I remain silent behind my smile.

"Later," I say as I leave. I'll call a realtor and start looking for an apartment today.

~*~

Max meets me at the jobsite. The Fergusons are his personal cross to bear. They're never satisfied, and they insist on working solely with my brother. That's what you get when you own the company, I guess.

"Great to see you, Brother." Max slaps my back.

"Ditto," I reply. "How's Maddie doing? I haven't heard an update on the twins for a while."

Max shakes his head. "She's tired and exhausted and we still have hopefully four months to go. She's never comfortable because one of the twins presses on her bladder all the time. We can't wait for these babies to arrive." Despite his complaining there's a lovesick smile on his face.

I don't ask for or want more details, but let's just say I'm happy for Max and Maddie because they want kids so badly. Maybe getting two at once will mean that Maddie only needs to do the whole pregnancy thing one time.

"So, Brother, how's the carriage house coming along? Shorty and Tom tell me that Miss Montgomery has developed quite a crush on you." The smirk on Max's face says it all.

I'll make sure to put way too much sugar in my crewmates' coffee next time I see them since they can't keep their mouths shut.

Playing dumb, I say, "Daisy is friendly to everyone on the crew, not just me. And the house is coming along nicely. You need to stop by."

Max nods, then a serious expression crosses his face. "Jacob, I have some advice for you. Don't waste too much time giving yourself excuses to avoid getting your heart broken. If you like Daisy, then ask her out. Maddie and I could have been married months earlier if we both weren't so stubborn and stupid."

"Well, I don't plan to fall off a roof, dislocate my shoulder, and break my arm in order to get her attention," I reply in a teasing voice.

Max shrugs. "That's exactly what I'm talking about. If I had told Maddie I loved her sooner, I wouldn't have had to go to such extreme measures." We both laugh.

My brother's fall off the roof was an accident, but it forced Maddie to wake up to the fact that she loved him. They got their happily ever after when Maddie proposed to Max in the hospital.

I consider Max's words. There's no doubt that I'm attracted to the feisty beauty. I've wanted her since the day she scolded us in that bikini. Maybe it's time to test the waters and ask her out.

A noise draws my attention to the front porch. Picky Mr. and Mrs. Ferguson have arrived, carrying tile and countertop samples. Lots of them.

"Oh boy, let the fun begin," Max says under his breath.

I head upstairs to frame the master bedroom closet, leaving Max to deal with the finicky couple.

Chapter Twelve

Daisy

Sylvie and Ford are enthusiastic to discuss the new business venture, but we've had a difficult time getting everyone's schedule to mesh for a face-to-face meeting. With the Fourth of July next week and all the family gatherings, everyone clears their calendar tonight for our exploratory discussion.

Gramps suggests that we meet here at their house. He and Grandma Erma attend the Chamber of Commerce meetings every Wednesday evening, giving us free run of the place.

"I'll make a light dinner for your friends," Grandma says.

I grin, knowing that means she'll cook a feast for us.

Sylvie arrives first. I squeal, pulling her into a big hug. My friend hasn't changed at all since we were college roommates. Her diminutive five-foot-four-inch frame is diametrically opposite to her giant-sized personality. The red curls, freckles, and mossy green eyes make her stand out in a crowd. Oddly enough, she has connections to Connor's Grove because her grandmother is Gretta Peterson who owns the campground off Highway 12. Sylvie used to work there in the summers.

"I haven't seen you in forever," she exclaims.

"Why did we wait so long?" I add.

Ford knocks while we're still chatting in the entry. He waves through the glass in the front door.

I wave back. "Come on in and join us."

He enters, pulling both Sylvie and I into one of his big bear hugs. Ford is as big as a grizzly bear with a full beard and deep voice. His nickname in college was Paul Bunyan.

I shoo my friends into the living room since we're still awkwardly standing at the front door. My hosting skills need a little work.

"Daisy, did you paint this?" Sylvie says with awe in her voice as she stares at my painting gracing one of the walls.

Walking over to stand beside my captivated friend, I say, "Yeah, it was my Christmas present to my grandparents." My nonchalant words contradict the pride swelling in my chest at Sylvie's reaction.

Ford joins us and shakes his head. "The painting is amazing. You're so talented, Little Bit." His use of my college nickname makes me giggle.

"Let's go out to the back patio. Jacob will be joining us soon." Embarrassed by all the praise of my artwork, I quickly accompany my guests to the patio where Grandma has already set up a luscious buffet. She even pulled out her long serving table for the occasion, saying the small patio table would be too crowded. The real reason is she made too much food.

Jacob spots us as he and the crew are shutting down for the day. I wave at him and he waves back. He loads his tools in his truck, then walks over towards us.

"That's Jacob?" The appreciation in Sylvie's voice is palpable. "Way to go, girl," she adds under her breath. I blush.

We all shake hands, with Ford and Jacob sizing each other up in friendly male fashion.

"Do you mind if I freshen up?" Jacob asks me. He has a clean T-shirt in his hand and a laptop bag hanging off his shoulder.

"Of course." I point him in the direction of the powder room. He returns in a few minutes looking fresh and smelling his usual spicy, woodsy scent. *I have an urge to snort his chest.*

"Grandma Erma went all out." I pull myself away from accidentally sniffing Jacob as I point to the buffet spread out on the long table. The guys mumble their approval in man speak and grab a plate.

We eat while getting to know each other. The guys discover they both were in the Minneapolis Curling Club and played several matches against each other.

"I thought you looked familiar," Jacob says to Ford with a snap of his fingers.

"Because of my impressive curling skills?" Ford makes a big show of flexing his biceps while Sylvie and I groan.

"I think it's the lumberjack look." Jacob snickers.

Both guys laugh.

After almost licking his plate clean, Ford turns to me. "Your grandmother is a terrific cook."

"Where did you put all that food?" Sylvie teases.

Ford pats his ample stomach then reaches for seconds. He must have a hollow leg because the rest of us are still working on our original servings.

Once everyone has had a chance to catch up with Ford and devour their food, the topic I knew would come up does. "Tell Jacob the story behind your name," Sylvie says as she elbows Ford. I've heard the story a hundred times, but apparently it's my friend's favorite. I think she has a crush on the big guy.

Ford rolls his eyes then turns towards Jacob. "Mom named all three boys after presidents. She said it would give us a good start in life to be named after such famous men."

Jacob's eyebrows draw together. "So, you're named after Gerald Ford I take it?"

The big man laughs and shakes his head. "Not quite. Everyone comes to that conclusion. I'm named after Rutherford B. Hayes. But when Dad held me for the first time, he said Rutherford was a ridiculous name for a baby and I've been called Ford ever since."

"I call him Rutherford when I'm mad at him," Sylvie adds.

Nodding, Jacob snickers, "I'll keep that in mind."

Tapping Ford on his shoulder, I say, "Tell Jacob the rest of the story." I know Sylvie will ask him anyway, so I want to beat her to it.

He grunts. "My other brothers are named Abraham and Ulysses. But they don't go by those names."

Jacob's eyes widen. "Ulysses does seem a little over the top."

Everyone nods in agreement.

"Mom's plan backfired as none of us ended up going by our legal names. My brothers said that the presidents' full names count and so Abraham is called Linc, short for Lincoln, and Ulysses is called Grant."

"Ha! Why aren't you called Hayes?" Mr. Connor replies with a chuckle.

The big man shrugs. "I like Ford."

Sylvie emits an unladylike belly laugh and punches Ford on the arm. Obviously, she's the person most amused by the story. "I'm going to start calling you Hayes." Ford glares back at her.

Once the dishes are cleared, I introduce the topic we're here to discuss. "As you know, I want to use my graphic design degree, applying it to commercial artwork for advertising and marketing." My friends nod in encouragement, so I continue. "Gramps has given me seed money, so we already have an operating budget. I estimate we can afford to pay ourselves modest salaries and cover expenses for about twelve months. With everyone working from home, we'll save money by not having to rent an office space. Once my carriage house gets done," I look pointedly at Jacob, "we can use it as our office when we need to get together all in one place."

"Impressive Daisy. I hadn't realized you'd planned this out so much already." Jacob's eyes flicker with respect while my friends smile and nod. A warm feeling washes over me as I delight in their admiration.

"Should we discuss what skills we each bring to the table?" Ford asks.

"Wait up." Jacob retrieves his laptop and starts typing. "If we're going to do this, we should do it right. I'll take notes. Go ahead."

All three turn to look expectantly at me. I guess this is my show. But Ford was the one who brought it up, so I gesture at him. "Well, Ford's specialty is marketing and copywriting for advertisements."

"I'm a master at writing a captivating hook, if I do say so myself." He mimics patting himself on his back.

Sylvie swats him on the arm. "And you're ever so humble. My area of expertise is market research. At my last firm, I was in charge of selecting the best media, like TV or radio, for our target audiences. I love conducting customer roundtables," she adds.

After typing furiously, Jacob jumps in to the conversation. "I prefer to work on project and budget management. And I like communicating with clients." He pauses and looks up at us. "Also, my brother is an attorney. He can draw up our company's official papers, client contracts, and other legal documents."

Ford gives him a high-five.

I smile at the way our team is already coming together. "I guess I'm the creative side of the team, although you can all help with creative input." While I plan to be lead graphic designer, Jacob and Sylvie have skills in that area and can pitch in as well.

"She's the best," Sylvie says before I have a chance to offer anything further. It's her turn to give me a high-five.

Looking at everyone's excited face, I vocalize my biggest concern. "Where do we start?"

There's a pregnant pause as we all ponder my question. I hope the others have some good ideas because I'm at a loss as to how to quickly get our name out there besides just creating a website.

Ford speaks first. "There's a charity gala in early September at the Minneapolis Marriott. My old firm always used to attend and I'm sure I can get us tickets. It's a good way to rub elbows with corporate types and network with decision makers."

"Great idea. My old firm used to also attend that. It'll give me a chance to reconnect with a bunch of my old contacts," Jacob says.

"We need business cards. I can design those," I chime in.

"And a company name. We're going to need one of those," Sylvie says with a laugh.

The rest of the evening is spent brainstorming a company name.

"How about St. Croix Designs, as an ode to our famous river?" Ford says while pacing back and forth on the patio and eyeing the desserts.

Jacob nods and scribbles it on the paper where we're putting down our ideas. We're using paper at my suggestion so we can visualize each suggestion.

"Mini Apple Designs," Sylvie adds. "An abbreviation for Minneapolis."

"None of us live in Minneapolis, you realize that, right?" I tease.

"Ah, but we want decision makers to think we're urbanites," Ford taps his chin while trying to look suave.

"So, Paul Bunyan meets the big city?" Sylvie says between giggles. The big man's lumberjack look simply doesn't give the impression he's a distinguished city dweller.

Jacob wisely crosses that suggestion off the list while Ford gives Sylvie a stink eye.

"Smart Design Agency," I blurt out, trying to take a new tack.

"We'll Help You Sell a Million." Ford snickers at his own suggestion.

"Hook 'em and Close 'em." Sylvie joins in the fun.

We all groan.

Silence settles over the group as we stare at the suggestions scribbled on the paper. None of the names are hitting us quite right yet.

Sylvie's apple suggestion got me thinking. "Cherry on Top Design Agency." I throw out the idea. "We can feature the iconic Spoonbridge and Cherry sculpture in Minneapolis as part of our logo."

"That's a clever tie in," Sylvie says.

"Plus, the suggestion that we're from the city might help open doors," Ford adds while he hovers beside Grandma's cake. I'm just waiting for him to swipe a finger in the gooey icing.

"Would we need to pay a royalty to use that?" Jacob asks.

"Good point. I'll research any royalty implications," I add, still keeping a close eye on Ford.

Jacob looks around the group. "Well, should we put it to a vote?"

"I vote for Cherry on Top," Ford says.

"Me, too," Sylvie exclaims.

Turning to me, Jacob raises an eyebrow.

"Of course I'm voting for my own brilliant suggestion."

Everyone laughs.

"Sounds like we have a consensus." Jacob types winning name into his notes, along with action items of checking on the royalty to use an image of the iconic sculpture and having his brother Quinn do a formal company name search. He emails everyone a copy of the document.

Ford rubs his hands together. "Let's celebrate with dessert." He turns towards the buffet table. "I'm ready for a slice of your grandmother's German chocolate cake."

We gather at the table with plates in hand as Ford starts serving up slices. Next time we'll have hot fudge sundaes with a cherry on top.

Chapter Thirteen

Jacob

After five months of construction, the carriage house is finally complete. Today I'm meeting Max there for a final walk-thru with Daisy and her grandfather.

When I pull up, Max's pickup is parked in the driveway. He gets out when he sees me. We exchange slightly awkward manly hugs even though we just saw each other last week.

As we walk to the front door, my brother rotates a full 360 degrees looking at the freshly installed landscaping and front yard. "I love the stone paver walkway and the fact that you added a curve to it."

"That was Daisy's idea," I reply.

Max stops for a second. "I'm excited I finally get to meet the delightful Miss Montgomery." His smile tells me that I'm going to get a lot of teasing after we leave. I've mentioned Daisy too many times in casual conversation with my brother—he probably knows about my crush on her. He'd have a cow if he knew about some of my "interactions" with Daisy.

"Gentlemen," John Vandervoldt says in his booming voice as he strides across the yard between the two houses. His fast pace belies his seventy years. I've decided that Vandervoldts age well, like a fine wine.

John and Max, then John and I, exchange firm handshakes.

"Shall we go on in? My granddaughter will be here in a . . . few minutes." He frowns at his watch.

Internally I roll my eyes, wondering why he's surprised by Daisy's tardiness. That seems to be her usual operating mode.

"The cleaning crew just finished this morning, so everything should be sparkling," Max informs us, sounding like a proud parent ready to show off his freshly bathed child.

We enter the great room and stroll around the cozy space. The soaring ceilings with dark accent wood beams make the room feel larger than it is. Gleaming wood floors and a modern see-thru electric fireplace turn the home into a showcase. The open floor plan provides just a teasing peek into the kitchen—part of the island and some cherry wood cabinets are visible, along with an eating area occupying a nook that juts out and overlooks the backyard.

"The house turned out even better than I envisioned. I'm very pleased with your company's workmanship," John says while we wait for his wayward granddaughter. He glances again at his watch and adds, "Daisy's in charge at this walk-thru. She's the one who needs to be satisfied. But please don't be put off if she's a little bossy."

Max laughs. "I've got one of those at home, so I'm used to it."

John grins. "I know the feeling."

Was Grandma Erma a spitfire in her day? Or maybe she still is. Guess it runs in the family.

We turn when the front door bangs open and a harried-looking Miss Montgomery walks in. Her auburn hair is windblown, and she has paint splatters on her T-shirt. But she still looks beautiful to me.

"Sorry I'm late. I was painting and lost track of time."

Mr. Vandervoldt chuckles and shakes his head. Daisy walks over to hug him tightly, barely coming up to his shoulder. Her love for the old man shines through her smile.

"Daisy, this is my brother Max." I motion towards my brother, just waiting for the usual female reaction.

Max strides over to Daisy and they shake hands. She smiles and giggles shyly at him, which is the typical response most women give my handsome, confidence-oozing brother. I feel a twinge of jealousy because I've always felt a bit like a second fiddle to both

Quinn and Max. They're successful entrepreneurs who own their own business. I'm a laid off advertising flunky who's doing part-time construction work and was living with my parents until a few weeks ago.

Pulling my thoughts back to the present, I watch the interaction between Daisy and Max. She catches my eye and winks. A happy warmth flows through my body knowing she's flirting with me and not my brother.

"Max, how's your wife doing? I understand you're having twins." Daisy says the part about having twins as if it's a dream come true.

A concerned look flashes across Max's face. "Maddie gets tired quickly. As you might know, she's a professor at the community college. Fortunately, she's finished teaching since the summer semester just ended. The doctor wants her to go on bedrest in a month. Twins tend to come early, but they're hoping to keep them baking for another two months at least. So, she's just subbing next month when other profs are out." He pauses and shakes his head. "My mom has already created a 'baby watch' schedule for her and my sister. She insists that Maddie not be alone. My sister-in-law sometimes comes over with her new baby, so the women can all spoil little Lilly."

Daisy nods. "I'm sure Jacob will keep me apprised of the baby watch." She gives me a pointed look.

"Of course. You'll be the first person I inform once the babies are born," I say with a bow and a little too much snark in my voice. Once we get Cherry on Top off and running, I should still see Daisy just as often as I did when the carriage house was under construction. John and Max try to hide their grins as they watch the dynamics between Daisy and me. She's always pushing buttons and I'm always pushing back.

Miss Montgomery's eye roll is directed at me. She quickly wipes that expression off her face and turns back to Max. "I'm ready for the grand tour. Looks like the cleaning crew did a great job." The wood floors that have been covered in about an inch of construction dust now look like they would pass my mom's white glove test.

Max accompanies Daisy as they walk around the house, chatting about the features and finishes. John and I listen but hang back, letting Max and Daisy set the pace.

When we enter the kitchen, the pair walk to the intricate backsplash. Max leans in for a closer look. "The glass tiles look fantastic, and whoever created the pattern did an excellent job. Random, yet pleasing."

Reaching out her hand, Daisy fingers the tile. Her lips twitch and a blush flushes her face. "I helped Shorty with the pattern. It was fun figuring out how to mix and match the sheets."

I roll my eyes internally at that understatement. My own face heats at the memory of her channeling of Meg Ryan.

"You have a real eye for pattern and color balance. Have you ever considered interior design?" Max's praise is met with a big smile.

"She *is* an artist," her grandfather adds with pride in his voice. "But don't give her any new career ideas."

Daisy's cheeks turn a darker red at her grandfather's teasing.

Since I've been mute almost the whole time, I chime in. "Miss Montgomery knew what she wanted, and she wasn't afraid to let us know."

Daisy punches me on the arm. Max raises an eyebrow and gives me a stern look. Oops I'm in trouble for riling up the client.

"I enjoyed assisting with the tile installation. It was challenging," Daisy says.

At this additional revelation, my brother glares over Daisy's head directly at me with a "you made the client help?" expression on his face. Feeling chastised, I squirm as I meet his gaze.

Putting my hands out in a mea culpa gesture and trying to placate Max, I say, "Miss Montgomery likes to be very hands on."

Max's frown widens but thankfully he lets the topic drop.

When we head upstairs, I start to sweat at what Daisy's going to say about painting the shower. Max knows how horrible that stuff smells and he'll wonder why I assigned the task to her. The trouble I'm in with my brother just keeps getting deeper and deeper.

Once upstairs, we first tour the master bedroom and Daisy's gigantic closet. I haven't seen it since Shorty completed all the painstaking work to construct hundreds of little compartments.

"I love the wall of cubbies," Daisy says as she excitedly points to the wall filled with the tiny cubicles.

"What are you going to use all those for?" Max asks.

She claps her hands and gives us an impish look. "For all my shoes. I have over five hundred pairs."

My brother and I exchange a stupefied look. *Who has that many shoes?* John Vandervoldt shakes his head and laughs.

"Oh Max, I want to show you how fabulous the tile in the shower looks." Daisy practically pulls him into the master bathroom. I hover in the background and she gives me a cagey grin over Max's shoulder. *Oh no, not a good sign.*

My brother turns back to me. "I assume you used the water-proof paint before installing the tile, right?"

Daisy's eyes widen and she starts to open her mouth . . .

"Yes, we did," my reply flies out in a rush to cut-off Daisy's comments. I throw in a firm nod, hoping to end this discussion.

Max chuckles. "That paint is the most horrible smelling stuff, but it's effective at creating a waterproof barrier." He then turns back to Daisy. "Hope you weren't here when they were putting that on, Miss Montgomery."

She smiles demurely. "I did get a little whiff of it."

As Max and John stride back down the stairs, Daisy whispers in my ear, "You owe me big time for not turning you in to your brother." She then flounces off, leaving me to wonder what price I'm going to have to pay for her silence. *Oh boy, the next batch of brownies might not be safe to consume.*

Chapter Fourteen

Daisy

Gramps insists on hosting a housewarming slash picnic slash potluck for the whole Vandervoldt clan. I think it's just a ploy for him to grill his famous onion burgers and brats, and for Grandma Erma to cook up a storm. But, hey, I roll with it. Grandma says to expect lots of tantalizing food from all the Vandervoldt women. I bake a batch of Betty Crocker brownies. Even though I burn them, I hope it won't be too obvious that I don't have the Vandervoldt cooking gene.

The fact is, I don't know my Vandervoldt family well, except for Gramps and Grandma. Mom never talked about family and she certainly didn't reach out to them. Not one time during my childhood was I introduced to my grandparents. When I moved to Minneapolis for college, I turned to Gramps only after I flunked out of school and had no other options. I'm embarrassed to admit how purely materialistic my reasons were for contacting my Vandervoldt grandparents. Now, I love Gramps and Grandma Erma beyond measure.

Big groups make me nervous, and the Vandervoldt family is enormous. At least sixty relatives live in tiny Connor's Grove, with many more residing in the surrounding areas. I've met a few of them but only in small batches, so this party is going to be overwhelming. It was always just Mom and me (and possibly one of her numerous boyfriends) for so long, I haven't adjusted to being in the large Vandervoldt fold yet.

My dread grows minute by minute. At least Gramps suggested I invite Jacob, so I'm looking forward to his companionship if I get overwhelmed by the family.

Jacob arrives early to help me set up folding tables and chairs around the backyard. He gives me a hug, which I wish was a kiss, but maybe I can get one of those later.

"The tables and chairs are in the basement," I say as we walk to the main house. Jacob waves to Gramps, who's doing last-minute weed whacking on a yard that's already meticulously maintained. Wouldn't want any stray blades of grass to overlap the concrete patio or driveway.

"Wow, how many tables do your grandparents have?" Jacob asks once we descend into the basement. Dozens of tables lean against the wall in neat rows, along with a handcart stacked full of folding chairs.

"I think they have around fifty, but Gramps said to only set up thirty. There's a fundraiser at the Methodist Church and some of the family are committed to attend that."

Jacob laughs then starts picking up tables. He pulls four off the pile.

I gulp as his biceps strain the confines of his shirt while he effortlessly picks up all four of them. "Can you carry all those?"

He grins. "This isn't a competition. You better only take as many as you comfortably can, even if that's only one." *How does he know me so well already?*

I grab two tables then proceed to drop one squarely on my foot. It clatters noisily onto the concrete floor.

"Ouch! Ouch!" I do an ungraceful hopping dance reacting to the pain, then I bend over and rub my wounded foot.

Jacob rolls his eyes, wearing an "I told you so" expression.

I point a finger at him. "Don't say anything, Mr. Connor. And certainly don't insult my choice of footwear."

He glances down at my strappy, open-toed sandals. The corner of his mouth quirks up and he shakes his head.

Hefting only one table, I join Jacob as we lug our loads to the yard where we set up the tables in the grass. We repeat this process several times, bringing out tables and then chairs until both Jacob and I are drooping with sweat.

"That should be enough," Grandma hollers at us from the patio. "Sit for a minute and enjoy some lemonade." She sets an ice-filled pitcher and a couple of glasses on the glass tabletop and waltzes back inside, probably to put the finishing touches on her cake. The condensation beading on the outside of the pitcher calls to me, so I make a beeline for the patio, limping a little from the injured toe.

I guzzle the lemonade down in an unladylike fashion. Jacob chugs his as well. When he glances over at me, I give him a lopsided grin.

"How's the toe?" As soon as the words escape his lips, his shoulders shake. He even wipes a few tears from his eyes.

"Are you laughing at me?" I grump.

"Um, no?" He coughs a couple times, but I swear it sounds like suppressed laughter.

My eyes narrow, but when I look down at my red toe, giggles burst forth. Jacob joins in the merriment as we laugh for several beats. I pour us each another glass of lemonade, which we sip quietly while we collect ourselves.

"Are you looking forward to the party?"

I pause then look left and right, ensuring that neither of my grandparents is within earshot. "Not really. I don't know hardly any of the family. Plus, they all know my mom's story, so some of them are probably coming just to see the black sheep's daughter."

He takes my hand and squeezes. "Once they get to know you, they'll love you."

Jacob's sweet statement touches my heart.

~*~

Guests start to arrive right as Gramps fires up the grill.

Every person who shows up says something to me, then moves on. All are bearing a tasty looking dish to share just like Grandma said they would.

"I'm your cousin, Johan." The giant-of-a-man smiles, then turns to Jacob who is standing beside me. "Remember me? We played city league softball together when we were in high school."

Jacob nods. "I'll catch you after lunch and we can reminisce."

Johan points a finger at Jacob, "You betcha." Then he yells across the crowded patio, "Who wants to play cornhole?" There's a scramble as enthusiasts rush towards the side yard where Gramps set up the game.

"That man likes his cornhole," Jacob whispers in my ear. I bite my lips and count backwards from ten trying not to laugh out loud.

When I turn back to the receiving line, I recognize my cousin Erik, his wife Amy, and their son Ethan, whom I've met several times before. Jacob's brother Quinn helped them with Ethan's adoption a couple years ago.

"Nice to see you Daisy. Ethan is so excited about Grandpa John's party. He's been asking us about it all week."

I bend down to address the tiny boy. His brown eyes stare solemnly back at me. "Ethan, Gramps said he's making a special hamburger just for you." He grins then hides behind his mom's legs.

As Erik and Amy move along, the next couple in line shake my hand. "We put out a big garden every year. In abooot two weeks, stop by for some tomatoes, beans, or cucumbers." The tall bearded man draws out his vowels, typical of most Minnesotans.

Even though I have no idea who he is, I smile at his accent and generous offer. "Fresh veggies sound wonderful. I'll take you up on that offer." The man's wife nods and they walk away.

"Who was that?" Jacob whispers.

"I have no idea," I whisper back. "But I'll ask Gramps so I can get some of those vegetables."

A lady who looks like Erik gives me a hug. "I'm Kirsten, Erik's sister. This is my husband Rolf." Rolf extends his hand and we shake. He's carrying a tiny sprite dressed in a blue princess dress, complete with tiara.

"You look so pretty," I daintily shake her tiny hand while she stares at me with her big, blue eyes.

"I'm Princess Elsa." Her voice is surprisingly loud for such a small person.

Everyone within earshot chuckles. "We can't get her out of that dress ever since we took her to *Frozen 2*, don't ya know," her embarrassed mom explains.

I nod, smile, shake hands, and exchange pleasantries as each person passes. There must be thirty-five to forty Vandervoldts here—not quite as many as Gramps predicted. Turns out Jacob and I didn't need to lug all those tables from the basement.

Once the family has politely greeted me and dropped off their culinary offerings, the buffet table is overflowing with all sorts of delicious-looking food—lime Jell-O mold, potato salad, baked beans in a crock pot, cheesy potato casserole snuggled into an insulated cover to keep the contents warm, and chips galore— potato chips with a side of French onion dip, tortillas chips with guacamole, and pita chips with some yummy looking hummus dip. My mouth waters at all the edible delights.

Gramps places an overloaded platter of hamburgers and brats beside the buns and all the necessary condiments—including homemade sauerkraut. The remainder of the table holds three plates of cookies, my slightly burned brownies, Grandma's cake, and two pies. We sure aren't going to starve.

Jacob looks over the loaded table and whispers to me, "And not a healthy salad in sight."

My eyebrows draw together, not familiar with his meaning.

He grins sheepishly. "Inside joke with my sister and me. Once you attend a Connor family dinner you'll understand."

A tingle spreads up from my toes to land in the vicinity of my heart. *I'd love to attend a family dinner with Jacob.*

Clap! Clap! Gramps gets everyone's attention. "We appreciate you all coming. Please enjoy the food. I hope everyone has a chance to meet our granddaughter Daisy." He waves and smiles over at me, so I wave back, too nervous to smile. "Afterwards, she'll be giving tours of the carriage house for those who want to see it."

A murmur goes across the crowd. I don't know if that's in reaction to meeting me or seeing the carriage house.

Hefty Johan Vandervoldt throws down his cornhole beanbag and rushes to be first in line, which breaks the crowd's hesitation to appear too eager. Everyone else follows while Gramps and Grandma greet their guests and urge them to eat lots of food. That isn't going to be a problem.

After Grandma serves her German chocolate cake, Erik and Amy ask to see the carriage house. Several other Vandervoldts stand to join us on the tour. Jacob winks at me as I lead the group across the lawn. I slow as we approach in order for everyone to take in the unique structure.

"This is bigger than I expected." *Were they expecting a tiny house?*

"Such an interesting design." Minnesota speak for they're not quite sure they like it.

"Good workmanship." Jacob's chest noticeably swells with pride.

Opening the front door, I motion for everyone to enter. "Come inside and look around."

The group immediately spreads out between the great room and kitchen. A few even meander upstairs. Vandervoldts aren't shy, apparently.

"Go show off the finishes." I push Jacob towards the kitchen where I hear oohs and aahs. He smiles and jogs away.

"You have so many shoes," someone shouts from upstairs. Two older ladies I don't recognize scramble up the stairs, mumbling something about Jimmy Choo. They must be fashionistas like me.

"Did you paint these?" Amy asks. Erik and she have paused in front of two of my paintings. Three other Vandervoldts join them.

As I walk over, I watch the different reactions to my bold, colorful painting style which doesn't always resonate with everyone. This set of pictures is an abstract rendering of cornfields and an old barn, shown in winter and in summer. They were inspired by Monet's art—he liked to paint the same scene in different seasons.

"I love these, Daisy. No wonder Gramps raves about your artistic talents," Amy smiles and her words are so ingenuous, they bring tears to my eyes. There isn't a jealous bone in this beautiful Asian lady's body.

Erik's sister Kirsten, who's standing beside Amy, squeezes my arm. "We're so happy you're living in Minnesota now. John and Erma just glow when they talk about you."

I blush and beam at her thoughtful comment. *Why was I worried that the Vandervoldts wouldn't accept me?*

Cackling erupts from the kitchen where the hunky construction guy is obviously entertaining the ladies. The noise breaks up our little artwork discussion, but I'll always remember the kind words from all my Vandervoldt relatives. Mom should have mended fences with her family a long time ago.

Chapter Fifteen

Jacob

Tonight's the charity gala we're attending to network for our new ad agency. Daisy is riding with me. Our other colleagues live in Saint Paul, so they're coming separately.

Daisy has been living in the carriage house for a month now. I park in the gravel driveway and again admire the S-curve pathway leading to the door. The curve was Daisy's brilliant suggestion and it looks much better than a straight walkway would have. She definitely has an eye for design. Hopefully that bodes well for our joint venture.

When I arrive, Daisy meets me at the front door. She's dressed in a tight black off-the-shoulder dress that sparkles when she walks. It hits her mid-thigh, showing off so much leg that my tongue almost falls out of my mouth. Impossibly high black heels round out the outfit. Every man in attendance is going to notice her, and it's going to be a long night trying to keep my hands off her.

"Come in," she says as she pulls me through the door.

"You look gorgeous." My fingers itch to embrace her and kiss her senseless, instead I lean in, whispering the compliment in her ear. She smiles.

Pausing, I take in the furnished carriage house. My heart swells with pride whenever I see the finished product. The contemporary vaulted ceilings have beams accenting the ceiling's height. The dark wood floors and cherry cabinets, white quartz counters, and open floor plan could be featured in *Architecture Digest*. A loft overlooks the great room. Even though the house is compact, it feels surprisingly spacious.

A brown leather sofa and loveseat sit at a 90-degree angle so the occupants can easily watch the flickering fireplace or 54-inch

TV hanging above it. Area rugs add warmth to the wood floors, and several of Daisy's incredible paintings grace the walls.

"I love this place more and more every day." Daisy clasps her hands over her heart. She must have caught me staring.

"It turned out even better than I expected. Quite an architectural masterpiece," I add, and she nods.

Mr. Bean trots up, asking for attention. Daisy scoops him up and we both pet him for a few minutes. When our hands accidentally touch, I feel the electrical shock tingle throughout my body. A pink blush spreads across Daisy's cheeks, as she reacts to the pheromones sparking between us.

I clear my throat, breaking the spell. "Let's go or we'll be late."

Daisy grabs a fancy shawl, wrapping it around her exposed shoulders. I mentally shake my head. *Get over it Jacob.* A pair of shoulders shouldn't give me heart palpitations.

~*~

The grand ballroom is decorated with gold and silver that glisten off the shiny black granite floor. It feels like we're in a Las Vegas casino but with high-end finishes.

Sylvie and Ford wave to us from a tall café table near the back of the room. Daisy and I wind our way over to them. A waiter takes our bar order as he rushes by. Our colleagues have a plate of hors d'oeuvres already sitting on the table.

Ford snags one and pops it into his mouth. "I don't know what these things are, but they're tasty," he says, making everyone laugh.

Sylvie and Daisy are busy complimenting each other on their dresses. Both women look stunning.

Ford leans towards me. "Daisy is turning heads. You better keep a close eye on her."

My eyes scan the room and see several men looking at our table. "I won't let her out of my sight. But I think Sylvie is also getting her share of attention."

His eyes widen as if he never considered that the petite redhead was also a head turner. I grin at Ford's clueless expression.

Once we finish our drinks and the appetizers, we scatter to mingle with the crowd, trying to connect with as many decision makers as possible. I keep Daisy at my side, hoping to ward off all the men staring at her. My jealousy surprises me.

A tall man with jet black hair strides towards where Daisy and I are standing. She sucks in a breath.

"Margaret, what are you doing here?" He asks, ignoring me.

I look at Daisy in confusion. Her clenched jaw and tight lips heighten my curiosity as to who this guy is.

"Hello, Father. We're here to make contacts for our new ad agency—"

He cuts her off with a dismissive wave of his hand. "You're still going to try that ridiculous venture? I assume Granddad Vandervoldt is financing the whole thing, am I correct?"

I want to punch the pompous expression off his face. He's wearing shoes that cost more than my entire outfit and his tie is knotted so precisely it makes me want to reach up and adjust mine to make sure it isn't askew.

Daisy doesn't change expression, nor does she confirm or deny his rude comment.

Turning to me, she clasps my elbow in a death grip. "This is my colleague, Jacob Connor. Jacob this is my father, Alec Montgomery."

He reluctantly shakes my hand. His cold, limp handshake doesn't endear him to me any more than his treatment of his daughter.

I put an arm around Daisy's waist, pulling her closer to me. I feel the need to protect her from her mean-hearted parent. She feels warm and soft against my body. Like this is where she belongs.

Looking down his beaky nose at her, he says, "You're just like your mother. Foolish, flighty, and full of fluff." He turns to me and adds, "She'll decide in six months that she's tired of this venture then be off to try something else."

Glaring back at him, I say, "Daisy's the creative brains behind our new venture. She's in this for the long haul." When I squeeze her waist, she steps even closer to me.

Mr. Montgomery sneers. "Just wait, young man, you'll see."

With that parting shot, he waves to someone across the room and strides away.

I frown at his retreating back. Tremors rumble through Daisy's body which is still plastered against mine. I wonder if her physical reaction is from anger or hatred or both. I know how I'm feeling right now.

"Excuse me, I need to use the restroom," Daisy says and rushes off before I can reply.

For several minutes my feet are glued to the floor. Suddenly so many things about Daisy make sense. I wondered how she could be so self-conscious about meeting her relatives when she's so obviously a lovable person. No wonder she feels that way, with a parent like that. Thank goodness she has her Vandervoldt grandparents for support. A parent should never treat a child like Daisy's father just treated her. Suddenly I feel so blessed to be a Connor. Even my meddlesome mom acts from her heart.

Spotting Sylvie, I quickly approach her. "Can you go check on Daisy? She went to the restroom."

Her eyes widen. "Is she sick?"

"No, we just had a conversation with her father."

Sylvie's lips purse into a hard line. "Say no more," she mutters over her shoulder as she strides towards the restrooms. By her reaction, Mr. Montgomery obviously has a reputation with her and not a favorable one.

Ford sees me standing by myself and joins me. I should probably ask him how his networking is going, but I can't shake the episode I just witnessed. Ford's known her a while, maybe he has some light to shed. "Do you know much about Daisy's father—Alec Montgomery?"

He smirks. "Other than the fact that he's a nincompoop?"

I laugh at the old-fashioned yet accurate description. Leave it to Ford to come up with the apropos term—revealing he's not a big fan of Daisy's father either.

Ford grins at my laughter. "Her father is president of Montgomery Enterprises. My old advertising firm had them as an account."

A lightbulb goes off in my head. My old agency also did some work for them. "You don't suppose Cherry on Top Designs could acquire some of Montgomery Enterprises' advertising budget, do you?"

Ford hoots and an evil grin lights up his face. "I know we can. Mr. Montgomery can help finance our little start-up." He slaps me on the back, "Brilliant, Jacob."

Mentally patting myself on the back as well and envisioning Alec Montgomery's surprise when he finds out he's bankrolled our venture, I add, "It will be so rewarding taking his money."

Ford grins and leans towards me so we can discuss our strategy for how to get a slice of the Montgomery Enterprises pie without being overheard by those standing around us.

~*~

Daisy is quiet for the remainder of the evening once she finally emerges from the restroom. Our big plan to make contacts was shot the minute Alec Montgomery showed up. But after my conversation with Ford, I view the incident with her father as having a silver lining.

I coax her into dancing with me on a few slow numbers. She smiles at all my jokes but doesn't offer too much to the conversation. She feels incredible in my arms, my attraction to her growing by the minute. But I've never seen her so withdrawn.

On the drive home, I ask the question that's been on my mind ever since the ill-fated interaction with her father. "Daisy, why does your dad call you Margaret?"

She sighs. "My given name was Margaret Daisy Montgomery. Margaret is after Father's mother. I never met her, but from all accounts she wasn't a nice woman. Daisies are Mom's favorite flower . . ." Blinking her eyes rapidly as if she's trying not to cry, she continues. "Once my parents divorced, Mom legally changed my name to Daisy Mae. The Mae part being after her mother— Grandma Erma's middle name is Mae. My father has always refused to call me anything other than Margaret. So my name was just another battleground for my parents."

Reaching over the seat, I squeeze her arm. "A child should never be a battleground, or treated like you were. I'm sorry, Daisy."

A tear trickles down her cheek and she shrugs. "My father's right. I start things and then lose interest. I'm always switching professions."

"Hey, you're going to stick with Cherry on Top. Ford, Sylvie, and I will make sure."

At least I get a small smile as a response.

When we arrive back at Daisy's house, the air between us turns a little awkward. Should I walk her to the door or just call it a night here in the vehicle?

91

"Come on in. Mr. Bean will want to see you again." Her pleading eyes make think that she doesn't want to be alone to ruminate over the incident with her father.

She's right with her prediction about the Chihuahua's enthusiasm because the minute Daisy opens the door, her dog circles our feet, yipping in excitement. I pick him up and look him in the eye. "Beanie, a gentleman is reserved and dignified," I inform the tiny creature. We stare at each other until he licks me on my nose. I suppress a laugh at how quickly my advice is ignored, then put him back down and he sits at our feet.

"He listened to you."

"Well I do have that kind of effect on women and dogs."

Daisy snorts.

"Do you doubt my effect on you?" The words rumble from my throat. I stroll closer at an unhurried pace, like a lion stalking its prey. My companion's eyes widen, and I watch her swallow. The chemistry between us flares higher with every step I take.

After valiantly fighting my attraction to her for several hours, my resistance crumbles. I pull her into a gentle kiss and a gasp initially escapes her lips, but after a second she participates actively. She wraps her arms around my neck, fusing every inch of her body with mine. The kiss turns from tentative to all-consuming. I try to show her without words what she means to me, trying to kiss away the horrible words said by her father.

When we finally come up for air, her hair is mussed, her lips are puffy, and her cheeks are an adorable shade of pink. I push a stray lock of hair behind her ear and then put my forehead against hers. A sigh escapes my lips. "I need to leave before this goes too far."

She nods, then picks up Mr. Bean, putting her nose into his soft fur. He blinks at me. I can just imagine the dog asking me if my behavior is how gentlemen act. *He's got a point.*

My heart is still racing from that amazing kiss, but I don't want to stand here like a silent idiot. I cast around for a topic of conversation. "Hey, remind me tomorrow to tell you about a game plan that Ford and I came up with while you ladies were in the restroom."

She looks up from cuddling Mr. Bean. "A game plan for Cherry on Top?"

I nod.

"Will it make us a lot of money?"

"If we play our cards right, it will."

She tilts her head, looking intrigued. I want to embrace her again and tell her about the scheme that should put a smile back on her pretty face. Instead, I grasp the doorknob, determined to not let her entice me any further.

"Jacob, thank you for standing up to my father tonight," she says quietly before I'm out the door.

I pause, looking back at her to see tears glistening in her eyes. "I'd stand up to anyone who treated you like that." It takes all my strength to walk away from her rather than try to sweep her off her feet. *Someday.* The door clicks shut behind me.

Chapter Sixteen

Daisy

Even though my father tried to ruin our evening, dancing and kissing Jacob was amazing. I fall asleep with a sappy smile on my face and dream of a hunky, brown-haired guy with incredible blue eyes.

I'm humming a love song while puttering around in the kitchen the next morning when my cell phone jingles.

"Sylvie, long time, no talk."

She laughs. "Right, has it been, like, eight whole hours?"

Looking at the clock on my microwave, I reply, "Almost."

"I'm checking to see how the night ended with Jacob. Any juicy details to share?"

Ah, that explains the phone call versus a text. Even though I love Sylvie, she can be a nosy pants.

"Nope."

"No fair, I'd share juicy details with you."

I snort. "He walked me to the door and acted like a perfect gentleman." *Except for the 6.5 magnitude earthquake from that kiss.*

"Somehow I don't believe you. I'll get it out of you eventually."

Snickering, I respond, "Was that the only reason for your call?"

"No. Ford wants to have a conference call with you, me, and Jacob; something about landing our first client. Do you have time tonight?"

"I'll check my busy schedule." I pause for a few beats. "Wow, it looks like I'm open."

She laughs. "Great. Tag, you're it to call Jacob."

"What time is the call?"

"7:00 p.m. We're doing a video conference call. Ford will email the link."

The line goes dead.

I chicken out and decide to text Jacob. I'm still a little shy from that nuclear kiss.

Daisy: Video call tonight at 7 with Ford and Sylvie, if you're available

My phone stays silent for several minutes. I wander over and pop a K-cup in my coffee machine when I hear my phone jingle.

Jacob: Sounds good. I've got a family dinner, but we'll be done by then

Daisy: Great. Ford is sending out the link

~*~

Later that evening, I get ready for the video call—making sure everything is set up on my laptop since I've never used the conference call software before.

Ding! Dong!

Who could that be? I'm not expecting anyone.

Mr. Bean rushes to the door and sits, anxious to greet our visitor. Laughing, I pull open the door to find Jacob standing there. My breath whooshes out at the sight of him—tight blue jeans, tight T-shirt, and scruffy beard. He is one sexy package.

"Surprise! May I come in?" The smirk on his face tells me he knows the impact he has on me.

"Certainly, come in. Mr. Bean is excited to see you." My giggle gives me away.

Jacob pulls me in for a quick kiss. It goes from zero to sixty in three seconds flat. And stops just as quickly. "That will have to tide you over until after the call," he says as he strolls into the great room, sitting his laptop beside mine on the coffee table facing the sofa. He pats the seat beside him, and Mr. Bean runs over and jumps onto the couch. Jacob shrugs. "I meant for you to join me, but Beanie has other ideas."

I put my dog on the floor and point to the corner. "Bed," I say in my firmest voice. It's a gamble as to whether he will obey me or not, but he obediently toddles over to his puffy dog bed by the end of the couch and settles in to watch the proceedings.

I join Jacob on the couch, and he gives me a wink. We each get on the video call on our own laptops to see Ford and Sylvie's smiling faces.

"Hey you two," Sylvie says and waves. She holds up a small figurine and wiggles it back and forth. I grimace, knowing what's coming next. "My latest acquisition in honor of Cherry on Top," she says with a squeal.

Both men peer closely at the screen.

"What in tarnation is that?" Ford says with the finesse of a bull in a china shop. Jacob and I chuckle.

Frowning, Sylvie replies, "Rutherford, I'll have you know that this is an exclusive, one-of-a-kind gnome. Grandma Gretta special ordered it for me. Isn't he the cutest?"

Everyone again peers through the screen at the red-hatted gnome sitting on a cherry.

"Get it? Gnome on Top instead of Cherry on Top?" Sylvie snorts and laughs so loud Mr. Bean runs from the room.

When we were roommates, Sylvie had gnome figurines scattered all around our room. Her grandma is the head of the Gnome Collection Club of America or something like that. My friend admitted to having 149 of these weird little figures but apparently that's just a fraction of the number in her Grandma Peterson's collection.

Ford ignores Sylvie's rapture over the red hatted cherry sitter and points to Jacob and me. "Are you two in the same room?"

Grinning, Jacob rotates his laptop until we're both in view. "Nice detective work, Sherlock," he says.

"Wonder what that means?" Sylvie says, jiggling her eyebrows. Jacob and I ignore her.

Ford clears his throat, ready to get down to business. "Jacob, will you take notes?"

My hunky companion turns his laptop back towards himself. "Yep, ready when you are."

Ford nods and launches into an obviously pre-prepared speech. "The reason for this call is Jacob and I propose that we go after the new advertising contract being bid by Montgomery Enterprises. They just put the RFP out yesterday and I got a copy from a friend at my old firm. It's an open RFP, meaning anyone can bid—"

My heart lurches at the mention of my father's company. A request for proposal is a serious step; do we really want to do this? I hold up my hand to cut Ford off. "We don't have a chance. My father will refuse to accept a proposal that I'm involved with. End of story."

Jacob chimes in, "He's not the primary decision maker in this case. It's a very lucrative three-year contract. Chances are slim your father will even know you're involved in Cherry on Top. At the gala, he never even asked the name of your new business. Ford will submit the bid on our behalf."

"I think it can work," Sylvie adds with excitement in her voice. "Plus, I can't wait to see your father's face when he realizes the truth."

"At that point, it will be too late for Montgomery Enterprises to back out without paying a large cancellation fee," Ford adds. He rubs his hands together but internally I hear him emit a villainous laugh. If Ford had a handlebar mustache, he'd be twirling it right now.

I bite my lip, looking at Jacob. He nods his encouragement.

Turning back to my laptop I say, "What if they do a background check on our company? My name is going to be on the LLC documents."

Shifting in his seat, Jacob replies. "We thought of that. According to Quinn, we can file the LLC paperwork solely under Ford's name. Sylvie, you, and me will be on the board of directors. But it can be a private board where the names aren't public. Once we win the bid, Ford appoints us to positions within the company and gives us full shares. We'd have a legal agreement beforehand, just between us, laying out all those terms and conditions in case Ford decides to run away to Mexico."

Ford laughs. "Very funny, Connor."

"You'd do that just so we can win the bid from my father's company?"

My three colleagues fist pump the air, shouting "Yes!" in unison. They've all witnessed at one time or another how Father treats me. He certainly hasn't endeared himself to any of them.

I grin. "Okay, I'm in. What do we need to do to win the bid?"

We spend the rest of the call divvying up tasks to complete the RFP. Jacob creates a timeline that we all agree to. "Team, I just emailed you the plan. I'll create a project management spreadsheet and start tracking progress tomorrow. But tonight, we celebrate."

Ford and Sylvie cheer and then sign off. Jacob snaps his laptop shut and pulls me closer. Mumbling against my lips, he whispers, "Now, where were we?" He proceeds to kiss me breathless. After a few minutes, I pull back.

"Did you want wine to celebrate? I have a bottle from the Vandervoldt housewarming party."

Jacob gazes into my eyes. "You're a pretty intoxicating treat, but I guess we should celebrate properly."

I hop up to retrieve the wine and cool off. We better slow this inferno between us down or we're both going to get burned.

After pouring the wine, we sit on the couch enjoying it while Jacob idly plays with my hair and massages my neck. Goose bumps rise on my skin at his gentle caress. His need to touch me indicates loud and clear where he wants this night to lead.

Taking a deep breath, I pull back from his touch and turn to look him straight in the eye. "Jacob, I'm not a casual fling kind of girl."

He pauses sipping his wine with a thoughtful look on his face. "So, what are you trying to tell me?"

I shift around on the sofa needing to get more comfortable for this soul-baring discussion. "After watching the parade of boyfriends coming and going in Mom's life, I vowed that I wouldn't take relationships so breezily. I want commitment before hopping into bed with someone." Anxiously pressing my lips together, I wait for his reaction.

He puts down his wineglass and pulls me closer. "Okay, you set the pace. We'll take it as fast or as slow as you want."

I smile up at him and he kisses me sweetly and reverently. We sit with his arms around me and slowly savor the wine.

Chapter Seventeen

Jacob

Over the next few weeks, the four of us work on the RFP like we've worked together for years. Once my construction job is done for the day, I join Daisy at the carriage house where we work until midnight on our pieces of the contract. I admit that while much of our time is focused on the task at hand, we spend a fair amount of time kissing on the sofa. It's getting harder and harder to leave her every night, but she hasn't given me the green light to spend the night with her and I'm not going to push.

Daisy is quickly erasing my initial impressions of her. She isn't the flighty bimbo I thought she was. The phrase "don't judge a book by its cover" applies to Miss Montgomery. A sexy package hiding a big brain. In my opinion she relies too much on getting what she wants by using her appearance. I catch her charming me with tight pants and shirts rather than having enough confidence in her intelligence to win me over with her words. Sometimes her actions aren't much different than the first day I met her, when she came sauntering over to the construction site in that skimpy bikini. I chuckle at the memory.

Now there's only four days to the submission deadline, which my project management calendar reminded me of this morning. I'm frazzled when I get to Daisy's place tonight because I put in a full day of manual labor on the Ferguson's house. They asked me about nine different changes before Max arrived to save the day. Although I'm too exhausted to work on the RFP, I have no choice.

When my cute colleague greets me at the door with a kiss, I feel a surge of renewed energy. She's wearing tight black leggings and a slouchy T-shirt that's too big for her. When she looks up at me, the shirt slips down off her shoulder, exposing creamy skin, then she pulls it back up. Once the process repeats several times, I become very distracted. Putting my lips on her bare shoulder, I kiss her and watch as goose bumps rise on her skin.

"Jacob, we have to work on the RFP," she reminds me in a breathless voice.

I sigh. Getting my laptop out, I join her on the couch. Mr. Bean hops up and tries to sit on my lap. Daisy puts him gently back on the floor.

We peer at the project management spreadsheet and each take one of the many items left to do. I note that on the document, so Ford and Sylvie don't work on the same thing.

Daisy brings in sandwiches and we eat while working on our laptops. She's sitting at one end of the couch and me the other. Mr. Bean lies between us.

Once my sandwich is consumed, I pause for a second, resting my head on the back of the sofa. The day's exhaustion hits me, and I drift off . . .

"Jacob," a recognizable female voice says as something jiggles my shoulder back and forth. I'm reluctant to open my eyes, so I try to ignore the nudging. "Jacob!" The louder, more forceful words pull me from my sleep. My eyes crack open and Daisy is staring at me.

I sit up and yawn. "Did I fall sleep?"

She giggles. "Yes, my company was too boring."

"Why didn't you wake me? I still have to get my task done for the RFP." A little panic and frustration seep into my voice.

"Settle down, Connor. I completed both tasks. Plus, you were too cute to wake up."

My pounding heartbeat slows down and I roll my eyes and stretch, trying to get myself fully awake. "What time is it?"

"Midnight," Daisy says. "I'd let you sleep on the couch, but Gramps will see your truck in the driveway and come over with a shotgun tomorrow morning." My companion must think she's funny, as she doubles over in laughter.

"You're right. I better leave."

Daisy slides closer to me on the couch and rubs the stubble on my cheek. "Afraid so. Even though Gramps doesn't have a shotgun, he's mighty protective."

I nuzzle my face in her neck and kiss her creamy skin. "You aren't making it easy to leave."

She nods, stands, and pulls me to my feet. *Not quite what I was going for . . .*

I tuck my laptop into the bag and turn to go.

"Maybe you should take off from Connor Construction for a couple days. You're burning the candle at both ends."

I yawn, supporting her point. "Max needs me. I'll be okay."

"Sweet dreams," she says blowing me a kiss as I shut the door. She's the sweet thing filling my dreams every night, and tonight won't be any different.

~*~

I purposely forget to set my alarm, assuming the morning sunlight will filter through my blinds and wake me. Instead, I sleep like a dead man . . .

Pound pound pound!

Glancing at the clock, I see it's already past nine o'clock and I'm an hour late to the construction site. Guilt sets in at my tardiness. Maybe I am burning the candle at both ends. *Is Max here to get my butt out of bed?*

Shuffling to the door, I open it without even looking through the peephole.

A smiling Daisy saunters in, carrying a carafe and a box adorned with *Connor's Grove Bakery* written in pink cursive writing. My mouth waters when I smell the aroma of fresh-baked goodies.

Miss Montgomery giggles when she looks at me. I try not to feel self-conscious about my pajama pants and wrinkled T-shirt that's been shrunk in the wash and looks like it's two sizes too small for me. I run my hand through my messy, bed head hair.

"You look yummy," she says. My eyes widen at the absurdity of her comment, considering my disheveled appearance. *Is bed head sexy?*

Walking into my little kitchen, she rummages through the cabinet for two mugs. "Come sit down. We'll share some of Mary Sue's delicious baked goods and get some caffeine in your system." *She sounds a lot like Mom.*

"I'm late for work, sorry, but I have to get going." The clock now says 9:10 a.m.

Daisy waves her hand. "No, you're not late. I called the office and talked to Max."

My brow wrinkles in confusion. "How'd you know my schedule?"

She puts her hands on her hips. "Well, let's see . . . You've mentioned your schedule about fifty times since we started on the RFP. Early mornings at construction jobsites followed by late nights on the proposal. It really didn't take a rocket scientist to figure this out."

Am I that transparent?

"Max was very understanding when I told him about your late night. You're supposed to be at the Ferguson jobsite by eleven. We have plenty of time." When I don't move, she points to the table where she's already sitting. "Park your butt in the chair and let's eat."

Grudgingly, I sit. "For a little thing, you sure are bossy."

My breakfast companion smiles. "I can eat all these pastries, if you don't want any."

"No chance, Little Bit. Hand me the bear claw," I wiggle my fingers, ready for the sugary confection.

Daisy's stunned look is priceless. "How do you know my college nickname?"

I grin. "I've learned a lot of things from Ford and Sylvie. It's surprising what those two will tell me when you're not around."

She blushes. "Fake news. Don't believe anything they say."

A belly laugh erupts from deep in my chest. I sip my coffee and enjoy getting my sugar fix for the day. Daisy is as sweet as the pastries and I crave her just as much.

~*~

I hate to admit Daisy was right, but the late start was exactly what I needed to get my energy back. My time at the Ferguson house flew by, and now it's time to wrap things up on the RFP. "Ford is submitting the proposal tonight," I say after Daisy ushers me in her front door and we exchange a heated kiss. "Is there anything you want to add?"

A slow smile crosses her face. "No, Mr. Project Manager."

"I'll give him the green light," I say as she tries to distract me by rubbing the stubble on my cheek and following it up with kisses. I gently push her aside. "Let me send this email and then I'll focus on you."

She nods, then sashays off to the kitchen. My nose perks up at the delicious aromas coming from that side of the house. "Something smells great."

"I cooked a celebration dinner, so hurry up, big guy."

That lights a fire under my butt, so I quickly crank out an email and send it off to Ford. I set my computer aside—thankfully I won't be needing it for the rest of the evening.

Daisy has set her small café table with a white tablecloth and china plates. We usually eat off paper, so these must be for special occasions. A white candle sits in the center, flickering as she moves around the table pouring red wine into the glasses at each place setting.

I walk over and kiss her neck. She turns in my arms, still holding the wine bottle. I remove it from her hand and set it on the counter. "Cherry on Top is off and running. I'm proud of you and how hard you worked on the RFP."

Her eyes widen at my unexpected praise. I need to remember to praise her more often because she's too used to hearing negative feedback from a certain parent.

"Why thank you Mr. Connor." She blushes and kisses me softly on the lips. As usual, the chemistry flares between us and the kiss turns passionate. I can't get enough of her. Groaning in my throat when she deepens the kiss, every cell in my body vibrates with desire. My blood rushes hot and fast through my veins.

Ding!

I pull back at the loud, intrusive sound.

"That's the timer for the lasagna. Are you ready to eat?" She gives me a coy smile then fans her face when she thinks I'm not looking.

"Yes." My voice sounds breathless, so I take a few calming breaths. I respect her and don't want to overstep her desire to keep our relationship on PG-13 footing, but it's harder than I thought.

She blushes as she goes to retrieve the incredible-smelling entrée from the oven. I see her taking slow, deep breaths—I'm obviously not the only one affected by our kisses.

Looking over at me, she adds, "Grandma Erma sent over some slices of German chocolate cake for us."

"A woman after my own heart," I tease.

Daisy swats me with a dishtowel. "Sit down Mr. Connor."

Once we're settled at the table, I hold up my wineglass for a toast. "To winning our first bid."

Daisy smiles and clinks her glass to mine, echoing my words.

I wanted to say "to winning your heart" but I remain silent. It's too soon in our relationship to have that discussion.

Chapter Eighteen

Daisy

We wait anxiously for a reply on the RFP, although we know there were several submissions and Montgomery Enterprises indicated it might take up to ten days to get a response.

Since the pressure of the submission process is finally behind us, our relationship has finally progressed to the dating stage. *It's about time.* Tonight, Jacob and I are going on a genuine, real-deal date. He wanted to take me to a fancy restaurant, but I opted for Joe's Pizza Barn—I can't resist their gooey, cheesy pizza. Afterwards, we're coming back here to watch a movie. I found a couple of good titles from Grandma Erma's romantic comedy collection that I'm sure he'll enjoy. Not. *I thought I was done pushing Jacob's buttons but obviously I was wrong.*

When we arrive at the pizza place, the entry is packed with teenagers, couples, and families. Jacob puts his arm around my waist, pulling me close beside him. "Wouldn't want you to get trampled." He smiles down at me. Standing beside Jacob, my head barely comes up to his shoulder. Just like when I stand by Gramps. *Why are Connor's Grove men so tall? Must be something in the water.*

I scan the crowd and see a man's head that I recognize. He stands out over the packed restaurant since he's quite a bit taller than everyone else. "Isn't that Max?" I say as I point.

The guy looks over the crowd and spots us at the same time. He waves then slowly winds his way through the throng with a small boy trailing behind.

"Brother, what are you doing here? Aren't you on baby watch?" Jacobs teases him once Max is close enough to hear over the hubbub around us.

With Maddie's approaching due date, "baby watch" is in full force. Jacob asked me to go with him last week, but I had volunteered to help Grandma Erma bake cakes for the after-church coffee hour. I plan on going next time so I can meet Max's wife.

Max slaps Jacob's back and shakes my hand. "Ash is with Maddie." Pulling the diminutive boy forward, he adds, "This is my mentee, Jamal. Jamal, this is my brother Jacob and his girlfriend Daisy." I blush since this is the first time I've been referred to as *girlfriend*. I like it.

The boy moves closer and I notice he has an awkward gait— must be the reason they moved so slowly through the crowd. "Nice to meet you." He shakes both our hands, then turns to me. "Are you named after the flower?" His serious brown eyes look me over from head to toe. This kid is grown-up beyond his years.

I laugh. "Why, yes I am. It was my mom's favorite."

Jamal nods. "My mom likes roses, but she says they're too expensive. Sometimes I pick her dandelions. We have lots of those around our apartment."

Max, Jacob, and I try to hide our amusement, but a few giggles slip from my lips. Jamal is quite the talker.

"We came to pick up some pizza and take it back to the house. Jamal's mom went to visit his sick grandmother in Duluth, so he's staying with us for the weekend. Would you two like to join us?"

Since this is my first official date with Jacob, I'd like to decline, but I look over at him for guidance. It's his family and I don't want to be rude. His arm tightens around my waist.

"Thanks for offering, but we're seeing a movie after this. I know Daisy's been looking forward to this particular film for a while," Jacob replies.

Of course, the small boy doesn't pick up on the excuse that we just want to be together. "Which movie Miss Daisy? I've seen a lot of them and can give you my opinion."

I discreetly pinch Jacob on his arm. Now I'm on the spot to think of a movie that's playing in the second run theaters around here. After a few seconds of racking my brain, I say, "We're going to *Little Women*. Jacob can't wait to see it either." I give my boyfriend a saccharine smile while he rolls his eyes.

Jamal frowns and shakes his head, black curls bobbing. "Can't help you there. That sounds like a chick flick."

"Actually it's a literary classic," I say primly, as if that changes the chick flickiness.

He looks over at Jacob, "Why do you want to see a girly movie?" The disgust in his voice is evident, and the way he ignored my literature comment shows how much use he has for that sort of thing, too.

Loud laughter erupts from my male companion and his brother. The affection on Max's face for the kid is obvious.

I bend over close to Jamal's ear and whisper, "He wants to sit in the back of the theater and smooch, so he doesn't really care what's happening on the screen."

"Gross," the squirt says while giving Jacob a thumbs down.

Jacob glares at me and Max laughs.

"Take out order for Connor," the hostess yells at the top of her lungs.

"That's our cue to leave. You two have fun." Max and his charge turn to get their order.

"Say hi to Maddie for us," Jacob adds. He then turns to me and gives me a stern look. "Good thinking on your feet Miss Montgomery. But I have no interest in watching a chick flick."

I giggle, knowing the movie selection waiting for us at home.

Love Actually . . . Pretty Woman . . . When Harry Met Sally . . . The Notebook.

Jacob's going to love them.

~*~

109

Joe's Pizza Barn makes the best thin crust pizza in the area. After three giant pieces of pepperoni, mushroom, and black olive pizza, I'm stuffed.

"Where did you put all that, Little Bit?" Jacob teases.

Darn Ford and his loose lips about my nickname. Swatting Jacob on the arm, I say, "A gentlemen never comments about how much a lady eats."

He snorts.

I blush, then defend myself. "I got distracted painting and forgot to eat lunch. So, this was lunch and dinner."

"A likely story." He nods with a smirk.

I roll my eyes and look for a new topic of conversation. "Jamal is the cutest kid. How did Max meet him?"

Jacob leans forward so he can be heard above the roar of the crowd. "Max and I are part of the Big Brothers organization. They pair mentors with kids in need."

My eyes widen. "How does Jamal fit in that category? He seems like a well-rounded kid."

Jacob takes my hand and plays with my fingers. "Jamal's mom wanted him to have a male figure in his life. His dad isn't around."

I can relate. My dad was never around. "Max seems to really like him."

"Yep. Max and Maddie treat him like their own. They fill in whenever Jamal's mom needs help. Plus, the kid's a sports fanatic, so Max has taken him to Twins and Vikings games."

I smile. Max and Maddie must have lots of love to go around. "Since you're also part of the Big Brother organization, do you have a mentee?"

Jacob nods. "Yeah, but he lives in Minneapolis. I connected with him when I still lived there . . . Funny you mention it, actually. I'm meeting Bobby next Saturday. Do you want to come along?"

I clap. "Yes, that would be fun."

"Okay, it's a date," Jacob says as he boxes up the remaining pizza.

On the drive home I realize I didn't even ask what the plans are on Saturday. I'm happy to spend time with Jacob no matter what we'll be doing.

Chapter Nineteen

Jacob

It's going to be interesting to see how a California girl reacts to the sporting event I'm taking Bobby to today. Daisy's bugged me all week for details, but all I told her was to dress warmly.

When I pick her up at the carriage house, she's wearing a red sweater that takes my breath away. The tight blue jeans add to my breathing difficulty. Daisy could wear a sack and look terrific in it.

She pulls me in for a quick kiss while Mr. Bean runs around our feet. The kiss lasts longer than the dog likes, so he starts jumping on my legs. We pull apart, laughing.

Bending, I pick up the little mutt looking firmly at his beady eyes. "It isn't polite to break up a kiss, buddy. Don't you know guy code?" He yips and licks my chin. I laugh as I deposit him back on the ground.

"Come on Beanie, to your bed." Daisy points to his bed and he runs over without hesitation.

"Wow, he's behaving better. What did you do?"

My girlfriend whispers behind her hand, "There's treats in his bed. He can be bribed with his stomach. Just like someone else I know." She winks at me.

Crossing my arms over my chest, I grumble, "Are you implying that I think with my stomach?"

"Um, yes . . . German chocolate cake? Lasagna?"

I shrug off the comment. *This woman loves getting under my skin*.

As I'm backing out of the driveway, Daisy asks, "So, where did you say we're going?"

I chuckle. "You'll find out in about an hour." *I know how to get under her skin as well.*

Daisy puts her arms across her chest and pouts. Good thing she dressed warmly.

~*~

Bobby lives in a run-down apartment complex near the airport. The sound of planes 24/7 makes the housing more affordable. He's waiting for us on the front step when we arrive, and he jogs to the truck.

My mentee is thirteen but looks older for his age. His six-foot frame hasn't filled out yet, so he's all skin and bones. He lives with his aunt and uncle. I've never been told the story about his parents, and he certainly doesn't talk about them.

"Bobby, how are you doing?" I ask once he's settled in the back seat.

"Everything's cool. And who's the beautiful lady?" Bobby is the quintessential Latin lover with dark hair, dark eyes, and an uncanny ability to flirt with women of all ages. And women of all ages respond to him in turn.

Daisy turns in her seat and extends her hand. "I'm Daisy."

Bobby takes her hand and slowly kisses it. Daisy's eyes widen at the unexpected move.

I chuckle. "Hands off, Bobby. She's mine."

He laughs. "Can't blame a guy for trying."

Daisy pretends to fan herself. Bobby laughs while I squeeze her arm. "Behave," I say under my breath. Miss Montgomery blinks back at me with an innocent look on her face.

Bobby settles back in his seat. "Can't wait to see today's matches. One of the teams is a contender for the US Olympics team. I think they're playing Sweden, so it'll be a tough contest."

"Yeah, I saw that on the schedule too. They're the second match."

Daisy tries to follow our conversation, but I see the confusion on her face.

"We're going to the Chaska Curling Center. Bobby's a big fan of curling—sometimes called chess on ice."

"Sorry boys, but the only curling I'm familiar with is for hair," my girlfriend says with a giggle. "But, I can't wait to learn."

Bobby and I exchange laughs.

~*~

The crowd is surprisingly large considering that curling is not a major sport. The bleachers are over half full and people are still arriving.

Bobby and I select seats near the center. Daisy sits on one side of me and Bobby the other. The high-profile game doesn't start until the current match ends, so this is a good opportunity to discuss the rules of the sport and answer any of Daisy's questions.

We watch the match between a team from the Saint Paul Curling Club and one that traveled here all the way from Japan. I lean towards Daisy, "Want me to explain the rules?"

She looks quizzically at the markings on the ice then nods. "Yes, please."

I point towards the action. "As you can see, each team has four players. The rocks they're sliding down the ice are called curling stones. Each stone is made of granite and weighs forty-two pounds."

Daisy gasps. "That heavy?"

Bobby leans over. "And the granite has to come from either Scotland or Wales."

"Granite is granite. They care where it comes from?" Daisy rolls her eyes.

We laugh at Daisy's comical expression. She'd care whether her clothes came from K-Mart or Nordstrom's, but I keep that thought to myself.

Ignoring her jibe about the source of the granite, I continue explaining the rules. "Even though they make it look easy, it takes a lot of practice and skill to control the stone and get it to land where you want it to. See the circular target near the end? That's called the house and is where they want the stone to stop. You score points by getting your stone closer to the center of the house— that's called the button."

Miss Montgomery bites her lips in concentration as she watches the action before us. "Why are they sweeping with those brooms?"

"The sweeping decreases the friction on the ice, which makes the stone travel in a straighter path," I explain.

Daisy nods, taking in the action and listening to Bobby's and my explanations. "They're wearing weird shoes. It's like they can slide on the one foot."

"Great observation," Bobby says. "One shoe has a Teflon sole, so it slides easily on the ice. The other shoe grips the ice so they can push off."

She leans over me speaking directly to Bobby. "Do you play curling, and do you have all this equipment?"

Bobby's eyes gleam and I can almost see the pride swelling his chest. "Yep, Jacob bought the equipment for me. He used to be a member of the Minneapolis Curling Club too." He grins directly at me. "I love being part of the club."

Daisy looks at me and mouths, "You're so sweet." A warmth spreads through my heart at her compliment.

She turns back to Bobby. "Do you own one of those heavy stones?"

He laughs. "No, the club owns the stones. I wouldn't want to lug one of those around."

"Me either." She giggles.

Somehow I've become like a third wheel as my girlfriend and Bobby discuss the finer points of the game. It's terrific how these two have hit it off—and I'm not surprised, knowing Daisy's big heart. I sit quietly, listening to the animated conversation and enjoying Daisy's interest in the sport. Bobby is obviously in his element explaining everything to a pretty female.

Once the match ends, Daisy tugs on my hand. "Can a girl get a hot dog around here?"

I put a grumpy expression on my face. "Am I just here to provide food?"

She laughs and pats my arm. "Pretty much."

I look at Bobby. "Want something from the snack bar? Miss Montgomery worked up an appetite watching all the action."

Daisy punches me in the arm.

My mentee stands. "Hey man, I'm always hungry."

I rise as well and glance down at my girlfriend. "You want to stay here or come with us?"

Daisy smiles. "You guys go get the food. I'll have a hot dog with lots of mustard and a Dr. Pepper."

"How about a plate of nachos to share?" I nod towards a hefty man in front of us who's snarfing down a plate overflowing with nachos smothered in cheese and hot peppers.

"Looks yummy. I'm in."

I smile and follow Bobby towards the stairs.

~*~

The match between the US Olympic hopefuls and Sweden is tied. Almost every seat on the bleachers is taken now. We sit crammed in like sardines, but I don't mind because Daisy's hip and leg is

116

plastered to mine. Every time she moves, I feel a tingle shooting down my leg. Even the molecules of air between our bodies are charged with electricity.

Daisy bites her fingernail as one of the US team members sends his stone down the ice. Two teammates furiously brush the ice as the stone heads right on target to the button.

"That's a great shot," Daisy whispers in my ear. I get a whiff of her vanilla-scented body wash. She smells so good that I'm surprised I haven't noticed this before.

We all surge to our feet and cheer when the stone slides to a stop right on the button. Daisy and Bobby lean over me and high-five each other. This is one of the rowdiest curling matches I've ever been to.

Daisy grabs my arm. "This is so much fun. I like the strategy of the game."

I put my hand on top of hers. "Are you glad you came?"

She stands on her toes and plants a quick kiss on my cheek. "Does that answer your question?"

I grin. Bobby elbows me in the ribs on my other side while the crowd around us shouts "Go USA!"

Chapter Twenty

Daisy

I've been recruited for baby watch today. Max and Jacob got called to one of the construction jobsites—some emergency with "the Fergusons" that needed their immediate attention. Jacob called me in a panic because his mom and Ash are visiting relatives in Iowa and Hailey is stuck at the Connor Construction office for a bit.

The Connors don't want Maddie left alone since she's in her final month. A pang hits my heart knowing how sweet the Connor family is and how they look out for each other. I never had that growing up.

I arrive at the designated time and Max greets me at the door. He's wearing his construction gear and ready to go.

"Daisy, come in. Sorry to impose on you, but I don't want to leave Maddie alone."

Grinning, I reply, "Max, it's my pleasure to help out. Thanks for asking me."

A beautiful black and white dog sniffs my feet. Bending down, I pet him. "Who are you? You're so pretty."

He wiggles at my compliment.

"That's Fibi. Maddie can tell you all about him—he's an Agility competitor. At least he was until a few months ago when Maddie couldn't do it anymore."

"I've never seen an Agility competition. I'd love to hear all about it."

Max motions down the hall. "Come on and meet Maddie."

We enter what must be the master bedroom. A beautiful woman is propped up with several pillows behind her back. She puts down a magazine she was reading when we enter. I glance at the name as it sits on the nightstand. *Journal of the American Mathematical Society*. That's some heavy reading.

Maddie holds out her hand and draws me nearer. "You must be Daisy. I'm so happy to meet you." She squeezes my hand. "Jacob talks about you all the time."

My eyes widen. "Um, well, you can't believe everything he says."

Maddie chuckles. "Don't worry, he has all good stuff to say." She motions to the guest chair beside the bed and I sit.

Max leans over and kisses his wife. He nuzzles her neck, and his love for her shines through his eyes. They exchange a few whispered words as he pats the huge baby bump. "Bye ladies. Have a good visit. Hailey will be here around noon." With that, he strides out of the room.

"Are you comfortable? Can I get you anything?" I ask as I wonder what topics of conversation Maddie and I are going to have in common.

She shifts in the bed as she sits more upright. I help her readjust the pillows then sit back down.

"Jacob says you're an artist and you helped design the carriage house they built. I'm impressed by all your talent."

I almost fall out of the chair. She's impressed by me? "I just recently started to try to sell my paintings. The Connor's Grove Artists Colony has a few of them for sale, but I've only sold a couple so far." The words rush out of my mouth before I can stop them. It seems rude to gush too much about my art with someone I just met, even though I have five paintings on commission, with one going to a well-known collector. "Gramps is my biggest fan and he has a couple hanging in his house." I shrug, trying to sound casual.

"Daisy, that's wonderful. Once I'm mobile again I'd love to see your artwork in person." She smiles. "Are you pleased with how your house turned out?"

I clap my hands together. "Extremely pleased. When Gramps and I found the design in one of Grandma Erma's magazines, we

119

knew that's what we wanted to build. It's more modern than a lot of homes in Connor's Grove."

"You helped with some of the interior finishing?"

I blush. How much does she know? "It was my chance to learn some new skills. Installing tile was fun and interesting. A certain painting task—not so much."

Maddie laughs. "Why?"

I lean closer. "Promise not to tell Max? Jacob would kill me if I told you."

The pregnant lady looks intrigued. She puts her finger to her lips. "I won't breathe a word." The way she whispers the words makes me think we're exchanging classified information.

"There was this terrible-smelling paint, like, truly awful that we had to apply to the shower as a waterproof barrier. Jacob assigned me the task. Let's just say that I tossed my cookies from the horrendous odor . . . And what's even worse is Jacob heard every stomach-emptying sound."

Maddie's face lights up and she leans forward, laughing like a hyena. The sound is contagious, and I join in. We're in stiches for several beats, both wiping tears from our eyes when the bout is over.

"Why did Jacob give you that task?" Maddie's voice is still breathless from our laughing binge.

"Um, we had a little competition going as to who could pull the biggest prank. Let me tell you, I called a truce after that."

We both howl with laughter again.

Ding! Dong!

I hop up. "Are you expecting company?"

"No, but it's probably my nosy neighbor, Gloria. Do you mind answering the door?"

Walking to the front door, I see a diminutive lady standing on the front porch. She's dressed like she's going to church—much too formal for a Wednesday morning.

I open the door only a crack. "May I help you?"

She peers through the opening at me. "I'm here to see Madeleine. I'm her neighbor Gloria." For such a small person, she's easily able to push her way in. The plate she's holding smells divine. Without invitation, she toddles off down the hall with me trailing behind. I'm not a particularly good bodyguard.

"Maddie, dear, I've brought brownies," Gloria declares as she enters the bedroom. "My, my! The baby bump has grown even bigger. You look like you've swallowed two basketballs."

My eyes widen in shock at the disparaging comment.

Maddie just laughs. "The babies keep growing and I keep expanding."

Gloria grins. "Well, that's a blessing in the sky." Maddie and I exchange a confused look at the mixed-up adage, but the petite neighbor barrels on, patting Maddie's hand. "How about some coffee and one of my award-winning homemade brownies?"

I wince inside at Gloria's comment since the only kind of brownies I know how to make come out of a box. And I usually burn them.

"I'm keeping away from coffee. How about a glass of milk instead?" Maddie turns to me. "Daisy, will you join Gloria in some coffee? She can brew a full pot."

"I never turn down coffee. Especially when chocolate is involved."

The perky neighbor claps her hands. "I'll go brew coffee and you stay with Maddie, dear."

Before either of us can respond, Gloria disappears.

Putting my hand up by my lips, I whisper, "Does she always take over like that?"

Chuckling, Maddie responds, "Yes. Always. She's like a walking whirlwind."

Personally, I'd hate it if a neighbor came in and made herself at home like that. Maddie has the patience of a saint. Plus, being under constant "baby watch" how does she get a minute to herself? I feel a little guilty at my own presence here.

When Maddie's cell phone rings, I excuse myself as she talks to Max. He's so sweet, calling her for an update even though not much has changed in fifteen minutes.

When I enter the kitchen, Gloria has everything under control. The coffee's almost done brewing and she's got matching mugs lined up on the island.

"I'm sorry but I never asked your name. I was too excited to see how the baby factory is doing," Gloria says with a cackle.

Clearing my throat, I say, "I'm Daisy Montgomery, Jacob Connor's girlfriend."

Her ears prick up like a terrier after a mouse. "You're Erma Vandervoldt's granddaughter? John and Erma are so proud of you."

I nod and blush at her effusive comments.

"Shame about your mother though." Gloria shakes her head and tsks. "At least you're back in the family fold."

Not knowing how to respond to either of those comments, I give a neutral head shake.

The tiny woman walks over and squeezes my arm. "Jacob Connor is quite a catch. Don't let that one get away." She even gives me a wink.

Again, I'm at a loss for words so I politely smile.

Once the coffee pot gives its final gurgle, Gloria loads everything up on a serving tray. The neighbor seems to know her way around the kitchen and the house. She gets a card table from the hall closet and sets it up at the foot of Maddie's bed then puts the overloaded tray on it. Maddie just smiles and lets her do her thing. An extra chair is hauled in from the dining room. All I can do is watch the tiny whirlwind at work.

Gloria reappears with a TV tray, which she positions beside Maddie on the bed since it can no longer fit across her lap. As if she's the hostess, Gloria puts the milk and two brownies on the TV tray. She then pours me a cup of coffee and hands me a brownie and does the same for herself.

Once we're all eating the delicious snack, Gloria picks right up on the conversation from the kitchen.

"How long have you been dating Jacob, Daisy?"

Boy is she ever nosy. "A couple months," I croak out over the brownie lodged in my throat. Once my throat clears, I add, "We're also colleagues in a new advertising company."

The tiny woman's eyes sparkle. "I love office romances. So many juicy opportunities to sneak in a couple kisses during the day. I found that the janitor's closet works best."

Sputtering, I reply, "It's not like that. We both work from home."

"That's a pity."

I look at Maddie for help. She just grins and continues eating her brownies. No help from that corner.

Gloria changes subject as quickly as she did when preparing coffee, giving me whiplash. There's no opportunity for a moment of silence as she starts to share details of an upcoming garage sale, complaining about all the work involved and that no one is willing to pay a fair price for second-hand items. I feel like interjecting and asking why she bothers to hold the sale, but my lips remain firmly pressed together.

After at least fifteen minutes hearing about the impending sale, my ears are bleeding. Maddie looks like she's zoning out, even though she nods at appropriate times throughout the soliloquy.

Gloria's talents obviously extend beyond coffee and brownies and include her gift for gabbing about nothing.

I tune back in when she says, "Charlie doesn't need any of that stuff anymore, so if it doesn't sell it's going to Goodwill." That's her final pronouncement about the sale (thankfully), as she pops up from her chair. "I better make sunshine while the hay grows." My brow wrinkles—something in that statement doesn't sound quite right but she says it with such confidence maybe I'm confused.

Gloria collects the empty mugs and plates, loads them on the tray, and disappears. You'd never know she was here except for the chair, card table, and TV tray she left behind.

She peeks her head in for one final comment. "Tell that sexy husband of yours hello." The door slams a few seconds later, announcing her departure.

Maddie and I look at each other, then I whoop in amusement. A belly laugh escapes from Maddie, which I hope doesn't induce labor. After several seconds of laughter, Maddie says, "See why Max and I call her The Tiny Gabbing Tornado?"

Nodding, I say, "The name fits in every way."

The image of Tiny Gabbing Tornado Gloria makes me giggle then start laughing harder. Maddie and I are still giggling and wiping our eyes when a pretty blonde carrying a beautiful baby walks in. "What's so funny?"

"Daisy just met Gloria."

The lady turns to me. "Welcome to the 'I've been bowled over by Gloria' club." She shakes my hand. "I'm Hailey, Quinn's wife, and this is Lilly Jean." She proudly shows off the baby bundled in a pink blanket nestled in a baby carrier. She carefully sits the carrier in the overstuffed guest chair. The baby snoozes despite our conversation.

A warm, snuggly feeling washes over me at the sight of the baby, turning me all mushy inside. "She's adorable. I wondered what her middle name was."

Hailey's eyebrows draw together in confusion. "What do you mean?"

"When she was born, I quizzed the construction crew for all the details—like name, weight, and time of birth. None of them could provide any information."

"Men!" Hailey says, shaking her head. "She's named after both our moms. My mom's middle name was Lilly and Quinn's mom's name is Jeannie. So we came up with the combination."

"It's a beautiful name," I say.

Hailey smiles, then turns to Maddie. "How are you feeling, sweetie? You're looking gorgeous with that pregnancy glow."

Her greeting is diametrically opposite to Gloria's greeting.

Maddie pats the side of the bed and Hailey sits. "I didn't realize how difficult the last few weeks would be. Even though I wasn't initially on board, the baby watch is really helping. Especially since I can't do much anymore other than run back and forth to the bathroom. Getting in and out of bed is becoming a challenge . . ." Her voice trails off, her lips wobble, and I see tears in her eyes. Being pregnant is no picnic, maybe I need to rethink ever having kids.

"Hey, every pregnant lady feels the same way. We're glad to help." Hailey then hugs Maddie and wipes the tears from her cheeks. My heart sings at the closeness of these two women. The Connors are a close-knit family.

"I'm sorry, the hormones make me weepy and feel sorry for myself." Maddie adds with another sniffle.

Hailey smiles. "No apology necessary."

Feeling like a third wheel, I clear my throat and stand. "I better get going."

Hailey pops up from the bed. "Please join us for lunch. I want to get to know you. Can you stay a little longer?" The encouraging smile on her face shows that she genuinely wants me to stay. When the baby carrier makes a little cry, she pulls out the sweet little girl and coos to her. "Would you like to hold her?"

I nod my head affirmatively, pleased that the new mom trusts me with her darling little girl. Hailey hands me the baby and I snuggle her in my arms. The precious bundle looks up at me with eyes as blue as Jacob's. She pulls her fist into her mouth and returns my stare.

"She looks good holding a baby, doesn't she?" Hailey says to Maddie.

Both women smile and nod. I blush.

Chapter Twenty-One

Jacob

We win the Montgomery Enterprises bid. I want to shout "take that Alec Montgomery" but instead I do an internal fist pump. Daisy's qualms about her father torpedoing our proposal seem unfounded at this point. Once the team settled down after the news (and after a few glasses of champagne to celebrate) I create a detailed project management plan and we're off and running on the first ad set due in six weeks. It's an aggressive schedule.

Daisy and I have gone out several more times—we enjoy the same kinds of movies, as long as we stay away from chick flicks. Our love of Asian food means we frequently visit Hunan Palace owned by Mr. Chen, who gave Hailey and Quinn their dog. One of the Vandervoldt cousins just opened a BBQ joint and Daisy and I were invited to the grand opening. Rolf's BBQ Smokehouse is a nice addition to Connor's Grove—I didn't know Norwegians knew much about BBQ, but Rolf spent a summer in Georgia learning the secrets of the trade.

My girlfriend was inaugurated into the Connor family by way of the baby watch. I was pleased that she wanted to help and was also relieved that Mom wasn't there. No need to throw Daisy to the wolves too early in our relationship. Maddie told me afterwards how much she enjoyed Daisy's company. She also retold the Gloria Robinson story, and she had Max and me in stitches. I can just imagine Daisy's face at the office romance comment.

Frankly, I do worry about mixing our business and professional relationships. Daisy is much more of a free spirit than I am in terms of how she approaches the Montgomery Enterprises project. She tells me that she's waiting for inspiration to hit, where I'd be cranking out ad designs even if they were horrible. The project management side of me needs to be making forward progress or I get anxious. I'm keeping my fingers crossed that she's making some progress on the ad campaign.

Today is the two-month anniversary of the completion of the carriage house and one-month anniversary of our first official date. I'm joining Daisy at her house for our team video call, and she's fixing dinner.

The auburn-haired beauty meets me at the door. Her hair is up in a messy bun and her shirt is spattered with paint.

"Jacob, come in. I have something to show you."

Her words are encouraging, and I assume she's finally making headway on our new advertising project. Pulling her in for a quick kiss turns into several minutes as we explore each other's lips. Daisy's like an addicting drug—I can't seem to get enough of her. When we come up for air, she rubs the stubble on my cheeks. "You're the best kisser, Mr. Connor."

Blushing at her comment, I let her tug me into the far corner of the great room where her easel is setup.

"The fall weather is such an inspiration. Here's my latest creation."

She turns the easel around, revealing a painting in bold orange, yellow, rust, brown, and blue. It's a scene of a lake much like the one we fished at, surrounded by gorgeous fall foliage. She's captured the way the trees reflect off the lake, giving the painting an ethereal look. The picture is stunning and it takes my breath away, but another part of me wonders why she's spending time painting when she needs to be doing the graphics design for the Montgomery Enterprises ad.

Unable to hold my tongue, words of disappointment spring from my lips. "You have time to paint but can't make any progress on the ad?" My voice sounds harsher than I intended.

Her face drops. "Don't you like the painting?" she says in a small voice.

I sigh. "Daisy, the painting is amazing. But you need to focus on Cherry on Top's business first. Painting should be your hobby." Right after I say those words, I realize that I need to pull my foot out of my mouth.

Daisy gives me another hurt expression and I see tears in her eyes. "I'm still having trouble finding my inspiration for that project."

Deciding to take a better tack, I say, "How can we help you? Can Sylvie give you some ideas?"

Daisy sucks in her lower lip. "It'll come. I promise to focus starting tomorrow. Let's not argue about his, okay?" Her pleading puppy dog eyes do me in.

"Okay," I say grudgingly. I don't want to fight with her, but my gut tells me that we're going to clash over this topic again. *Why can't she make progress on the campaign? Is it because she's afraid to disappoint her father?*

Her face brightens and she beams at me. "I made tacos for dinner. We can eat right after the conference with Ford and Sylvie." She takes my hand and pulls me to the couch where I set up the call on my laptop.

The rest of the evening goes smoothly because Daisy and I ignore the elephant in the room. But how long can we pretend it doesn't exist?

Chapter Twenty-Two

Daisy

Once Ford delivered the hook and ad copy for the Montgomery Enterprises project, I tried and tried to come up with a design for the ad that compliments Ford's killer blurb. At first I was too surprised and giddy that we won the contract to really focus. But now I've been working on the project for a couple weeks and have started several times without success. I'm beginning to get a little panicky. The deadline looms only three weeks away. It's like I have writer's block, only it's graphic designer's block.

Ding! Dong!

My heart drops at the noise. Jacob is here to review progress on the design, and I have nothing to show him. Again. It's a repeated theme from the last several times he was here. I get the vibe loud and clear that he's frustrated with me. I'm frustrated with myself.

"Hey, Daisy," he pulls me in for a quick kiss. We don't linger like we usually do. He's all business tonight.

Plopping on the sofa, he open his laptop and waits for me to join him. I sit down slowly, knowing that I'm going to disappoint him yet again.

He squints at the very familiar project management spreadsheet, then looks at me. "I thought we'd review your designs. Can you pull them up on your computer?"

Biting my lip, I turn towards him. "I don't have anything new to show you. I don't have a handle yet on the vision for the ad. But it will come soon." I try to reassure him with a forced smile and false enthusiasm in my voice.

Jacob sighs and sits back, folding his arms over his chest. "Daisy, what do you need so you can move forward with the design? What else can we do to help you get the *vision*?" He says the word vision in a snide voice and glares at me for a response. I can almost see the smoke coming out his ears.

"I'll come through. I promise you. Give me a little more time to work on it."

A frown meets my words. "We have a deadline to meet! Put on your big girl pants and grow up. There's no safety net to catch you this time. It's almost like you want to crater this project." He spits out each word and they each hit me smack in the chest. This argument is going to kill both our personal and business relationships with one shot.

The harshness of his words surprises me. But he's not wrong. I'm falling back on my typical behavior of quitting before I even get started. My mind churns with emotions as I try to figure out what to say to appease him. But I'm not fast enough.

Jacob stands, snaps his laptop shut, and strides to the front door. "You have two weeks. In the meantime, I'm also assigning the design to Sylvie. We'll see who can create *something* before the deadline."

I stare at him. Mr. Bean emits a growl at the grumpy human glaring back at me.

Jacob points his finger. "No more excuses."

"I'm not making excuses; I just want my design to be perfect." My raised voice sounds like a toddler having a tantrum.

"What design?" He snarls back.

My lips snap shut as his comment hits its mark. I have no comeback to the truth.

Jacob pinches his nose and shakes his head as if he wants to say more, then the door slams shut behind him.

My mouth hangs open in shock. I guess this is why it isn't wise to date your colleague. Our business and personal relationships are too intertwined. And I just blew up both of them. This sure feels like we just put the last nail in the coffin for our relationship—an all-out breakup. A few tears leak from the corner of my eyes. Mr. Bean hops into my lap, licking my chin. I look down at him. "I guess it's just you and me again. Like always." His little black nose twitches and he snuggles into my chest. Jacob just took a chunk of my heart with him and it may never heal.

A therapist would probably have a field day with why I'm not making any progress on this project. Am I afraid to fail? Or is it I'm afraid to succeed?

~*~

I toss and turn all night after the ugly scene with Jacob. My eyes are red and puffy from my crying jag.

Sylvie's face lights up on my cell phone as it dances across my desk. I sigh and pick up.

"Hey," is all I can muster as a greeting.

"You're all rainbows and sunshine this morning," my friend replies.

I grunt. Luckily, she can't see me—she'd be shocked at my appearance. I'm wearing ratty sweatpants, a T-shirt that hangs on me like an oversized bag, my hair is in a messy bun on my head, and I didn't even bother to put on lip gloss, let alone makeup.

She continues, not discouraged by my silence. "What's up with Jacob assigning me the Montgomery Enterprises graphic? He said that we're both going to submit a design to Ford and him in two weeks. You're a much better designer than me. What gives?"

My loud groan cannot escape her notice. He really did it? I wondered if his threat to get Sylvie involved was just spoken in a heated moment and that he wouldn't follow through. "I've got a creative block and haven't shown anything to Jacob in a couple weeks." I pause for a minute, thinking about whether to share what happened yesterday. Why not? She'll find out anyway. "Jacob and I had a big fight last night. He stormed out when I couldn't show any progress."

Sylvie's sigh echoes through the line. "Generally I'd take your side, but I can see it from Jacob's standpoint. He's the project manager trying to get us to a deadline." Her gentle tone helps alleviate the sting of her veiled criticism.

"I know. But he was livid . . . I just wrecked everything." A huge sob escapes and the waterworks begin.

"Daisy, Daisy." I can mentally see her shaking her head. "You're a brilliant designer. I'm not worried that you'll come up with something spectacular."

"Try telling that to Jacob," I mumble between sobs.

"Actually, I did, but he didn't listen. He said that he's assigning me the design like an insurance policy. Just in case."

My heart drops. "Wow, he really doesn't trust me."

Sylvie laughs. "Honey, can you blame him? This is his first project working with you. Plus, there's a lot riding on this from a company standpoint. He's a little stressed out."

"I know," I mumble.

"Just do your magic and produce a rock-star design."

I smile at my friend's encouraging words. "Okay, I better get started."

"That's the spirit . . . And, Daisy, you didn't wreck everything."

My brows draw together. "What do you mean?"

Sylvie chuckles. "Let's just say that our project manager was pretty upset about the fight."

"He said that to you?"

"Not in so many words, but Jacob was really down when he called to assign me to the Montgomery project. He sounded like his dog just died."

Sighing, I beat myself up for the hundredth time for failure to deliver and backing Jacob into a corner.

"Daisy, once you deliver, all will be fixed. Believe me."

I stare at the phone for several minutes after she hangs up. *Wish I had as much confidence as she does in my ability to create an amazing design and to win Jacob back.*

Chapter Twenty-Three

Jacob

Team conference calls over the next week are awkward, and I rush to get each one completed as quickly as possible. Stony silence reverberates between Daisy and me. Our customary fun banter is replaced by short, terse answers to any question I ask her. She's businesslike, and I miss her usual flirty, goofy self.

I can't seem to figure out the line between Daisy's and my business and personal relationships—it's mixed up in my mind. Which means even though I'm annoyed at her, I still want her with every fiber of my being. On top of that, losing my temper at her was an unprofessional move and something that I deeply regret. The guilt weighs on me when I see Daisy's pinched face on every call.

After one particularly tense call, Ford pings me on my cell afterwards. I reluctantly pick up.

"You gonna tell me what's up between you and Daisy? You two are as frosty as the north pole."

I grunt. "She hasn't shown me any progress on the ad design for several weeks. We had a blowup over it."

"Ah, I wondered why Sylvie was suddenly also working on a design."

I plead my case. "You guys are all depending on me to lead this project to the finish line. That's what I'm doing."

Ford blows out a big breath. "I realize that, Jacob. But from previous experience, I know we can count on Little Bit. She'll come through with something that will blow your mind."

Daisy must have impressed Sylvie and Ford on other projects the way they both defend her. "Maybe. But, in case she doesn't, we'll have Sylvie's design as backup."

He laughs. "Just wait. Daisy's going to amaze you." Ford signs off, but his words don't make me any more confident that the alleged design genius is going to come through.

~*~

At least I've got a family dinner coming up, so I don't dwell 24/7 over the breakup with Daisy. I've fallen into a dark funk over what I thought could be a lasting relationship. I miss Daisy's funny comments, her sweet smiling face, her radiant beauty, her outlook on life, and most of all her kisses. Despite my anger and disappointment at her inability to create a graphic design for Montgomery Enterprises, I still want her.

"How's the new apartment?" my sister Ash asks when I arrive.

I perk up at her words, taking my mind off the puzzle that is Daisy. "I really like it. Quinn passed along the Connor furniture castoffs that Hailey had in her apartment, so I'm not sitting or sleeping on the floor. But," I lean closer to my sister and say in a low voice that Mom can't hear, "that ugly flowered sofa's gotta go. I'm donating it to Goodwill next week."

She snickers as we walk into the kitchen where the smell of Mom's pot roast tantalizes my nose.

Nana and Hailey are busy pulling food out of the oven. Quinn is sitting at the island holding baby Lilly. He's tickling her tummy and she's giving him a toothless grin. Dad and Granddad are discussing something yard related on the back patio—I see them pointing to the raised garden beds which are no longer producing since it's so late in the season. I smile at the contented, happy sight. I can't believe I missed so many of these when I was working that stupid job in Minneapolis. *Wish Daisy could be here with me.* That thought wipes the smile off my face, knowing that she may never attend a Connor family dinner. During my many deliberations over our relationship this last week, I've decided that we can't go

136

back to dating if we're going to make our new business successful. A personal relationship is out of the question. Now I almost don't want our business to succeed . . .

A noise draws our attention as Max and Maddie walk in. She's so big she waddles, but Max looks at her like she's the most beautiful woman on earth.

Mom appears and fusses over Maddie. "Sit down, dear. Those babies can't come too soon."

The pregnant mom plops awkwardly in one of the chairs at the island. "You are spot on with that statement, Jeannie. But we still have at least three weeks to go."

Max pulls her into a hug and rubs her lower back. "Mom, this will probably be our last family dinner until the babies arrive. Maddie's doctor put her on full-time bed rest starting next week."

All the Connor women huddle around Maddie, clucking over her while saying encouraging words. Quinn, Max, and I exchange a look that says we're happy we don't have to bear children.

"We'll bring the next dinner to your house," Mom declares enthusiastically. She pulls open the patio door and yells "Dinner's ready!" even though Dad and Granddad are standing right there. I shake my head because some things never change.

Everyone helps carry food as we move the party to the dining room. Hailey positions Lilly's baby carrier so she can see us while we all sit down.

"Join hands and we'll say the blessing," Mom says.

Since we all know the drill, we clasp hands around the table while Mom says the Johnny Appleseed prayer. When we don't have company, Mom falls back on the same prayer every time. Hailey says she's going to get Mom a book that has lots of dinnertime prayers, so we don't have to hear the same one all the time. Sounds like a good Christmas gift.

Ash reminds me to try some of her latest "healthy salad" concoction. Even though I can't identify a thing in it, I take a scoop to pacify my sister. Where's the lime Jell-O salad? She never brings that. Maybe I need to have Mom sneak Ash the recipe. When Max winks at me across the table, I nod to the meager portion of the weird salad on his plate and he smirks.

"When do we get to meet your girlfriend? You know you can invite her to our family dinner any time," Mom blurts out.

"She's the Vandervoldt's granddaughter I hear," Nana adds.

I almost spit out the bite I just took. Taking a quick sip of water to wash down the food, I look up to see all eight pairs of eyes staring at me. Only baby Lilly is ignoring me while she plays with the bottle that Hailey just gave her.

"We broke up," I say.

"What?" The shocked exclamation comes from Hailey and Maddie. Ash just snickers like she expected this news. Considering both our shaky dating histories, her reaction isn't unwarranted.

"We had a disagreement about a work project. End of story."

The Connors all exchange disappointed looks. After this announcement, Mom's going to start trying again to match me with a daughter of one of her friends. I recognize the glint in her eye.

After we eat in silence for a few minutes, Dad says, "That's why you never mix business with pleasure, Jacob."

Looking over at Dad, I laugh, and the table joins in. My dad is Captain Obvious.

Chapter Twenty-Four

Daisy

The only person I can turn to for advice is Gramps. He'll know what to do. I meet him for morning coffee on the patio. We won't be able to do this too much longer with the weather turning colder every day.

"Why so glum?" Gramps asks the minute I arrive.

I flop down and pour my coffee. I need to caffeinate before having this discussion. Gramps waits patiently while I take several fortifying sips. "I have a creative block on the ad I've been working on. Jacob and I had a big fight over my lack of progress. We haven't spoken for two weeks." Tears roll down my cheek as I say the words. I hastily swipe them away with the back of my hand.

Gramps nods, looking surprisingly unsurprised. *Am I that predictable?* "And what do you think is holding you back from making progress?" His kind blue eyes look over at me then swivel back to his mug. The silence hangs between us, but my grandfather doesn't seem to be worried about it. The lull encourages me to come up with an answer.

I squirm in my seat. This is the same question I've been asking myself for weeks. I know the answer, even if I haven't wanted to admit it to myself—or Jacob. "I'm afraid I'll disappoint the team. I'm afraid I'll fail to come up with something amazing." A little voice inside me adds *I'm afraid to disappoint my father yet again.* Knowing that ultimately this ad campaign is for my father is freaking me out.

Taking another sip of my coffee, I watch Gramps do the same. I know that he likes to thoroughly think through something before he speaks, unlike me. So I patiently wait for his response.

"Daisy, seems to me that you're already disappointing the team. Isn't an average design better than nothing?"

I gaze down into my coffee mug as if it holds the answer, then I look back up at Gramps. "But I want the design to be incredible and blow his socks off."

"Who's socks—Jacob's or your father's?"

He hits the nail on the head. I stare back down at my coffee. "Both," I mumble.

My wise grandfather drums his fingers on the table, drawing my attention back to him. "Kiddo, here's what you do. Today you're going to produce three designs. Even if they're terrible, you get them created in that fancy software you use. I'll come over tonight and we'll talk about each one."

A smile lights up my face. Finally, a game plan I can grasp on to. "I can do that."

He chuckles. "Well, get going. I'll be over after dinner."

~*~

The day flies by as I create designs. Ford's catchy hook line plays over and over in my head. I start to see how my graphics support the concept, and that there's more than one possible way to play this. I create a humorous version, a serious version, and an edgy modern version. By the time Gramps arrives, I'm ready.

"Okay, show me what you have." He sits beside me at the big monitor on my desk, and I pull up the first design. It's cartoonish and funny but has potential.

Gramps squints at the screen. His neutral expression doesn't let on what he's thinking. "Tell me the pros and cons of this one, in your opinion."

I trail my finger along a bright red section of the design. "Too colorful, looks a little amateurish, and the customer might not take the product we're advertising seriously."

A proud smile at my honest assessment crosses his face. "True, but surely there are some positives to this one."

Squinting at the flashy design, I laugh. "This one is playful and whimsical. Probably not what the client is going for though."

Gramps belts out a huge laugh, knowing my father would never produce a product that could be even remotely described as playful and whimsical. "Let's see the rest of them."

We walk through each design, with me listing pros and cons. By the time we're done, I know which one is the winner.

"Well, are you ready to show something to Mr. Connor?"

I nod happily. "I'll show him all three, but the second one is the winner."

Gramps smiles and nods his agreement.

I hug the wise old man. "Gramps, thank you for helping me. I was paralyzed by fear that I'll disappoint, like I always do."

His loving eyes widen at my words. "Daisy, you have never disappointed me or Grandma. We love you very much and are always proud of you. I wish your mom had let us get to know you sooner. We wasted a lot of years over that feud. Don't let that happen to you."

My eyes glisten with tears. Gramps has never expressed his disappointment over missing my childhood to me before. His double meaning doesn't escape me—I need to end this feud with Jacob right now.

"I suspect that your young man will come around quickly. He's in a tight spot with the deadline staring him in the face."

I shake my head and sigh. "I'm the one who cratered our relationship. Just like I always do."

Gramps takes my hand. "It's not too late to fix it. Don't run away or quit because you're scared. Go to him and show him how he can rely on you and how amazing you are."

My self-doubt dissolves at my grandfather's insightful words. No wonder he's such a successful businessman. Smiling, I commit to repairing the situation with Jacob as soon as possible. I'm not going to self-destruct this relationship if I can help it.

My beloved grandfather stands, unfolding his tall frame from the chair.

"Thank you, Gramps," I say as I hug him one more time.

He pats me on the back. "You just needed a little push. You did all the work." He winks and walks away.

~*~

Even though it's 11:15 p.m., I drive over to Jacob's apartment. No more delays or hesitation on my part.

A sleepy, disheveled, grumpy Jacob answers the door. "Daisy, why are you here?" His frosty welcome doesn't sound encouraging and it makes me want to turn around and flee, but I don't.

I wish I could fall into his arms and beg for forgiveness. Instead, I push my way inside and say in my most professional voice, "I have three designs to show you for the Montgomery Enterprises ad." I snap open my laptop and sit on his new leather couch.

He yawns and sits beside me. His cranky expression doesn't deter me from my mission.

I pull up the first cartoonish-looking design and talk him through it. He hears me out, then says, "I don't like it." His blunt words don't even hurt because he's right. That design won't work.

Nodding, I say, "I agree."

When I bring up design number two, his eyes light up and he sits up straighter. I have his full attention so I barrel on. "This one captures the features of the product and supports Ford's hook line perfectly. I think it still needs a little tweaking, but it has potential."

He grabs my hand that's pointing at the screen. "It's perfect, Daisy. I wouldn't change a thing."

"You think so?" My excitement leaks through as I say the words.

"I know so."

We gaze at each other. He's still holding my hand. I see something in his eyes that I haven't seen in a while—wonder, happiness, and delight. My heart sings with joy.

"I was scared to disappoint you with my design, but I disappointed you anyway with my procrastinating. I'm sorry." I look down in embarrassment and shame.

Jacob puts his finger under my chin, raising my eyes back to look at him. He smiles, squeezing my hand and making my heart think we can put this bump in the road behind us. "How did you get over your creative block?"

"A wise old man told me that he believed in me. He said even if I produced an average design, it was better than nothing. That was the push I needed."

Jacob nods. "Mr. Vandervoldt is brilliant."

"And incredibly supportive. I needed someone to tell me that getting the job done was better than getting it perfect." I try to cushion my words so they don't sound like criticism. But frankly, now that I'm over my wallowing in self-pity, I'm still angry about how Jacob handled everything.

He clears his throat and adjusts his position beside me on the sofa, indicating to me that my words hit home. "Daisy . . . I'm sorry that I didn't believe in you, but I panicked—"

I put my finger over his lips. "I fell back into my usual behavior of self-sabotage. My father was right about me always quitting when things get tough."

My colleague points to the screen. "But you didn't quit this time. Why not?"

Leaning over I kiss him on his cheek and whisper, "Because my need to make you happy overcame my fear of failure." *And overcame the fear of disappointing my father.*

He gazes back at me for several minutes as an awkward silence falls between us. He shakes his head as if he's made an internal decision. "Daisy, as much as I want to pick up our relationship where we left off, that's not a wise decision. We obviously can't date and work together."

Say what? Jacob's statement takes the wind out of my sails. I jerk my head back as if someone slapped me. Where did this crazy idea come from? My heart drops like a rock and my stomach hurts.

"Listen, we both want Cherry on Top Designs to be successful, right?"

I nod but not with much enthusiasm.

"We can still be friends, but our business relationship needs to take priority."

His words strike my heart like a gunshot wound to the chest. One mistake and I've already blown my chance with Jacob? Is there no way to fix this?

He stands and I have no choice but to follow.

"I'm so proud of you for coming through on the design, Daisy. What you created is amazing, and our client is going to love it. Put it on the shared drive and I'll let Ford know it's ready to send to the customer."

His all-business tone makes me grit my teeth. Well, I can play the same game.

"I'll have it on the drive as soon as I get home. Goodnight, Mr. Connor."

When I look at him over my shoulder as I head to the front door, I see sadness in his eyes for an instant and then it's gone.

Chapter Twenty-Five

Jacob

Ford submits our creative package to the Montgomery Enterprises advertising director with one day to spare. His innovative hook and ad copy, Daisy's incredible graphic design, and Sylvie's proposed media rollout are going to blow the director away. I sigh in relief that it's all over. We won't know the reaction to our package for a few days, as the advertising director wants to review it with her staff. Team Cherry on Top is anxiously waiting for the results.

My decision to keep Daisy's and my relationship as a business one sounds more and more stupid every day. Each time I talk to her, I want to tell her that I didn't mean what I said and beg for forgiveness. I berate myself for my terrible decision to keep her in the "colleague-only" box, yet I'm hesitant to change anything. Will we just have another blowup next time a deadline is looming and she hasn't produced anything? It feels like a catch-22.

Ford has provided his blunt opinion several times in private. My only defense to his arguments is that I want our little company to succeed and that's my focus right now. But my heart can't help agreeing with what the burly man said to me last week: "If you want a personal relationship with Daisy badly enough, you'll make it happen. Quit being an idiot."

Thankfully, I can keep my mind off the conundrum of Miss Montgomery because today I'm working on the mansion for Connor Construction's celebrity client. We're all on our best behavior because the homeowner is in town and wants to review progress with the team.

Everyone on the crew had to sign an NDA because the client is a professional football player, well known in the community. He doesn't want the people of Connor's Grove to be snooping around the jobsite. Or know his new address.

Brock Steele is the tight end for the Los Angeles Rams. Local boy made good. We all wished he had signed a contract with the Vikings, but the Rams snapped him up in the first round of the draft before the Vikings had a chance at him. He lives in California during the season but wants to spend the off-season in Minnesota where he can fish, canoe, and hike. Max told me that the abundant outdoor sporting opportunities are why Brock selected a secluded waterfront property on the St. Croix River. Since the guy's a billionaire, he can afford the hefty price tag for the prime location.

Brock and I went to high school together. He was a star on the football team, while I was a star on the lighting crew for our stage productions. Basically, our paths rarely crossed. My sister Ash had a huge crush on him. They went out a couple of times, but I never understood why they broke up. When I knew him, Brock was a stand-up guy. Everyone in school liked him, and he treated everyone with respect even if he was a football legend. Years have passed and he now earns an outrageous amount of money, so I don't know how that has affected his attitude. I guess today I'll find out.

"Gentlemen let me introduce our client, Brock," Max says when the two men arrive at the jobsite. Even though my brother is well over six-feet tall and muscular, Brock is at least a head taller and much bulkier. He looks like he could pick up a Cadillac and sling it over his shoulder. The guy has muscles the size of boulders. No wonder his nickname on the football field is "Man of Steel." *How many hours of weightlifting does it take to stay in that kind of shape?*

Luke, Shorty, Tom, and I trade handshakes with Mr. Steele. His firm grasp makes my hand hurt and I understand why he's one of the best receiving tight ends in the league. With that grip, it's surprising he ever drops a pass.

"Nice to meet you guys. Jacob, I remember you from high school."

My eyes widen. He's the same, down-to-earth Brock I used to know. "Yeah, I think we had World History together, right?"

Brock laughs. "Was that the class taught by crazy old Mr. Woodson? I think we called him Pattern Blind Woodson. Some of his clothing combinations made my eyes hurt."

Chuckling, I say, "His green and red plaid jacket with those navy blue corduroy pants was my favorite."

Even Shorty and Tom are laughing since they both know Mr. Woodson and his reputation for horrendous outfits.

Max clears his throat, wanting to get back to business. "Brock, how do you want to do this? Should we walk around each room and discuss any changes?"

"Sure, I'd like that."

With clipboard in hand ready to take notes, I trail behind Max and Brock while they discuss changes. Shorty, Luke, and Tom return to work on the guest house out back. It isn't far enough along for our client to walk through it today.

When we get to the kitchen, Brock sighs. "I wish that I hadn't listened to Tiffany about that backsplash. It looks like something you'd see in one of those million-dollar, flashy motorhomes."

Max pauses and a glimpse of a smile crosses his face. "Do I take it you're no longer with Tiffany?"

Brock grimaces. "I'd rather forget that lapse of judgement on my part. Also, I'd like to remove all reminders of her from this house." He looks directly at Max and me. "Sorry to cause you guys extra work. Just charge me whatever it costs to make the changes." Most clients aren't this amicable about spending money, but thousands to him are like dollars to us mere mortals.

"We want you to be satisfied," my brother says in a firm voice. "So, back to the tile." Max points to the backsplash. "Do you want to review some samples, or do you have a style in mind?"

The big guy wanders closer to the area under discussion. "How about a simple white subway tile? Don't you think it will look good, and pop against the grey and white counters?"

My brother nods his agreement to the proposed change.

Wow. Mr. Steele knows more about design than I thought he would.

He must notice the expression on my face. "I dated an LA interior designer for three months. She rubbed off on me." He shrugs.

Max and I laugh while I scribble the change down on the list.

As we walk around the house, there's only a few more areas which were "Tiffanied" as Brock calls it. He points out the tile in the master shower, which we will also replace with the subway tile.

When we get to the master bedroom, Mr. Steele looks like he's blushing. His gaze is directed at the mirrored ceiling above where the king-size bed will sit. He mutters, "What was I thinking to agree to that?"

I bite my tongue to keep from laughing out loud.

"Do you just want us to remove the mirrors and re-drywall the ceiling?" Max asks.

The blush on Brock's face gets even darker. "Yes, please remove that monstrosity as soon as possible. Thank you." He strides off to the master closet like his butt is on fire.

Max whispers to me, "Guess he isn't the playboy we thought he was."

Chapter Twenty-Six

Daisy

I'm determined to gain Jacob's confidence in my ability to deliver on schedule and at the same time blow his socks off with my creativity. That's the only plan I can come up with that might convince him that we can have both a personal and a business relationship.

Mr. Bean and I are sitting on the couch. Me with my laptop on my legs and he sitting on my feet. Even though my dog's tiny, he's like a mini heater for my always-cold extremities.

My computer dings with a reminder about our team video call meeting in five minutes. Since I'm still in my PJs, I scramble into the bathroom to comb my hair. Sitting back down, I say to my dog, "Think they'll notice my Miss Kitty pajamas?" He wiggles his black nose but remains quiet about the cat depicted on my clothing.

Ford, Sylvie, and Jacob's faces all pop onto the screen. We wave at each other, then Jacob runs the meeting. His business-like demeanor sometimes gets on my nerves. Some days I want to tell him to get the stick out of his butt.

"I'll share my screen and we can discuss the next set of checkpoints for Montgomery Enterprises' second project. But first, Ford wants to give us an update on our first delivery."

Ford's face becomes the focus on the screen as he talks. "Charlotte Zwick, Montgomery's advertising director, called me this morning. She loves the design we submitted for the first deliverable. In fact, she raved about it and feels that we captured in words and graphics the 'essence of the product.' Her words not mine," he says with a grin. "She's going to show Daisy's graphics to Alec Montgomery because she thinks he may want us to use that style for the rest of the product line. This could be huge!"

I gasp. Father is going to see my design? My hands start shaking, so I clasp them in my lap.

"My name isn't on the design, right?" I blurt out, panic leaking through my voice.

Jacob chimes in, "No, but don't you think it would be good for him to know what a rock star you are in the graphic design field?" His sweet smile hits me square in the heart. I want to shout *remind me why we can't date?*

Instead, I shake my head vigorously. "I don't want my father to know. He'll hate the design if he knows who did it."

Several seconds of silence greets my words as my colleagues absorb what I just said.

Jacob finally speaks. "If that's what you want, but personally I think you're making a mistake to remain anonymous."

Ford and Sylvie nod in agreement.

"I know my father. He might even break our contract if he knows I'm involved—just to be spiteful."

Everyone drops the topic and I simmer in embarrassment and anger at my heartless parent.

"Moving on to the project plan, looks like the next deadline is in two weeks. Daisy, can you give us an update on the graphic piece?" Jacob says.

I grind my teeth at his overly professional tone. Sitting up straighter on the couch, I say in an equally business-like manner, "I'll send out the design to all of you to review tonight. It might need a few tweaks, so I want to get your input as soon as possible."

"That's our girl," Sylvie says in an enthusiastic voice. She's always my biggest cheerleader.

"Um . . . well, nice job," Jacob says as if he's having trouble with his words. He's obviously shocked that I'm ahead of schedule.

Ford laughs. "Little Bit, you always amaze me."

Now if I can only get Jacob to say that. *Maybe someday.*

150

~*~

One day later, I'm enjoying some solitude and painting time when my phone rings. It dances across the table and I'm tempted to ignore it. When I see Jacob's before-the-breakup hunky smile on the screen, I'm really tempted to ignore it, but I don't. *Reminder to self: change photo to Jacob's post-breakup business only frown.*

"Hello?" My voice sounds frosty even to me.

"I can tell you're thrilled to hear from me," Jacob says with a lot of snark.

"Not so much. How can I help you?" I say this in my most professional voice. I can act just as businesslike as he can.

"Daisy, can't we please be friendly colleagues?"

I snort. *Think again buddy.* "Yes. This is me being friendly but professional, Jacob." I enunciate "professional" very clearly.

He groans. "Okay, well, I'm calling to let you know that Charlotte Zwick contacted me this morning. She said that Alec Montgomery loves the design and wants to chat with the designer. She insisted that I give her your contact information so she can set up a time for a call with him."

"You didn't tell her who I am, did you?" I fling the words back at him, the urgency evident in my voice.

"No, that's why I'm calling you . . ." He pauses for a few beats and clears his throat. "Daisy, I think you should take the call with your father. He should know what a talented daughter he has."

I sigh, then plop down on the couch and Mr. Bean hops into my lap. I stroke his soft fur while I carefully choose my response. "Only bad can come out of any conversation with Father. Tell Charlotte the designer politely declines a call with Mr. Montgomery."

Jacob exhales. "Daisy, are you sure?"

"Yes, I'm sure. My paints are drying out on the easel, I need to go. Goodbye." With that, I end the call. A couple tears roll unchecked down my cheek. The two men I'd most love to have a relationship are staying firmly at arm's length. One by my choice and one by his choice.

~*~

Ding! Dong!

Who can that be? Since we had our team call only two days ago, it can't be one of my colleagues. As much as I'd love to see Sylvie, I'm not in the mood for company.

I shuffle to the door, hesitant to open it. Gramps or Grandma always call first before coming over. I have no other neighbors, and the girl scouts aren't selling their yummy cookies yet.

I slowly open the door, ready to politely tell whoever it is to leave. My mouth drops open. Alec Montgomery is standing on my porch. His gray suit and red tie look appropriate for the board room and not for a casual visit to his daughter. Come to think about it, when has he ever visited me before?

"May I come in?" My father shifts back and forth on feet encased in Berluti oxfords, costing over two thousand dollars a pair. *Even my Manolo Blahnik's don't cost that much.* I'm not sure I've ever seen him look nervous before.

Holding the door open wider, I motion for him to enter. Mr. Bean growls at him, so I pick up the protective dog.

Father and I stare at each other for a few minutes as if neither of us knows what to do or say next.

I wave towards my leather sofa. "Do you want to sit down?"

He sits, making sure not to muss his thousand-dollar suit pants. He'll probably send them to the dry cleaners after this visit. Due to dog hair and all.

152

I settle onto the love seat across from him. Mr. Bean trembles in my lap as if he's ready to attack our visitor at any moment. The Chihuahua acts like a sixty-pound dog rather than one that barely weighs in at ten.

My father glances around the room. He can't miss the tasteful furnishings and stunning artwork on the walls.

"You have a nice place here, Margaret. I like it."

I almost fall off the love seat. What? No snarky comment about the bright colors in the artwork? No snide remark about the fact that Gramps paid for the place?

Mr. Bean growls in the back of this throat. Father sits back in his seat as if he wants to put the most distance between him and the tiny guard dog.

I swallow my surprise and try to respond as pleasantly as I can. "The carriage house turned out really well. Gramps and I came up with the design, and a local Connor's Grove construction company built it." Let's see what my snotty dad thinks about those comments.

"Ah, well, they did a great job. Looks like quality workmanship."

I narrow my eyes. "I'm sure you didn't come here to discuss my house. What is the reason for your visit?" It's getting harder to hide my feelings, and the words come out sounding harsh.

The mighty Alec Montgomery shifts in his seat. He looks uncomfortable. I feel a twinge of guilt. *Dang him!*

He clears his throat. "I had a most enlightening conversation with Jacob Connor this morning. Miss Zwick put me in touch with him when she couldn't find out who did the design for our product line."

My heart races in my chest. I take a few calming breaths. "What does that have to do with me?" Maybe Father is here because he's playing a hunch. If I play it right, he won't find me out.

He continues, "Mr. Connor was very reluctant to reveal who did the design. He said that the designer wanted to remain anonymous. He didn't give you up, Margaret. I made an educated guess. You see, I didn't forget about our little encounter at the charity gala a few months back. So, I put two and two together."

Now it's my turn to squirm in my seat. Keeping a poker face, I reply, "How did you know where I live?"

My diversionary tactic doesn't work. In fact, it brings a smile to Father's face. "I called up John Vandervoldt and had a conversation with him as well."

Darn the men in my life. Can't they keep their mouths shut?

My dad leans forward. "Daisy, did you do that outstanding graphic that has everyone in my company in raptures? It's one of the best designs I've ever seen in my thirty years in the business."

He sits quietly while I blink furiously at the tears threatening to roll down my cheeks. A lump the size of Texas forms in my throat. It doesn't escape my notice that this is the first time he's ever called me Daisy. And the first time that I've thought of him as Dad. All I can do is nod.

When I look closely at my dad, I see tears in his eyes as well. He looks away for a minute, then clears his throat. "I'm proud of you," he says quietly.

I stare at him, not believing what I'm hearing.

"I've been a terrible father. I don't deserve your forgiveness, but can we try to forge a relationship? I need to get to know my brilliant daughter." He points to my artwork scattered around the room. "I assume these are all yours, too?"

"Yes," I say in a small voice.

He shakes his head. "I let my opinion of your mother leak into my relationship with you. Daisy, I'm sorry." Standing, Dad adds, "I know you need some time. Forgiveness can't come in only minutes after the way I treated you for years." He hands me his business card. "Please call me when you're ready."

When he gets to the front door I say, "What really changed your mind? Surely it wasn't just my design?"

He looks back at me and I see sadness in his eyes. "When I questioned Mr. Connor about whether you were the designer, he told me that I didn't deserve a daughter like you. Then, when I spoke to your granddad, he said that you make him proud every single day and that I should open my eyes."

A smile crosses my lips and the tears I had held at bay slowly trickle down my cheeks.

"You've got two men who think the world of you. I want you to add me to the list *someday*."

The door latch clicks loudly, then he's gone.

~*~

My computer chirps the next morning, reminding me of the Cherry on Top video call commencing in five minutes. It's our weekly call but I'm not particularly looking forward to it. Maybe the team won't find out about my visitor from yesterday.

"How's everyone?" Ford's smiling face is the last one to arrive.

Sylvie and I wave at him while Jacob gets right down to business. His serious expression makes me want to salute.

"I just received an email from Charlotte Zwick. Let me read it real quick and see what she wants."

My stomach drops, but I keep a neutral expression on my face.

Jacob's eyes scan the email, then widen. He looks directly at the screen. "I'll read this part to everyone . . . Mr. Montgomery met with the designer yesterday and is looking forward to future designs from her and the Cherry on Top team."

There's silence for a few seconds, then Sylvie launches an interrogation. "How did he find out who the designer was?" Sylvie huffs as she glares at the screen. "Ford, did you open your big mouth?"

"Hey, it wasn't me," Ford says while holding up his hands in a placating motion.

My friend is like a mother bear whose cub is threatened as she starts in on Jacob next. "Someone on the team obviously squealed . . . Jacob?"

I wave at the screen, getting everyone's attention. "Hey guys, no one squealed. My dad figured it out."

Three faces stare back at me with obvious questions and concern on their faces.

"So, what happened?" Sylvie finally asks.

"Um, well . . . he apologized for assuming that I'm just like Mom. He wants to have a relationship with me when I'm ready." I wipe a few tears from my eyes. "It was a lot to process and I'm still reeling."

Sylvie blows out a small breath. "Oh sweetie, that is a lot of take in."

Ford and Jacob both commiserate by nodding.

Screeeech!

A blaring, high-pitched noise splits the silence. Mr. Bean flees upstairs to escape the deafening alarm.

I put my hands over my ears and jump to my feet. "My cookies!"

Rushing into the kitchen, I grab hot pads and snatch the smoking pan from the oven. Twelve black chocolate chip cookies stare forlornly back at me. I plop the baking sheet on the island, retrieve a dish towel and wave it back and forth at the smoke detector that's still trying to wake the dead. After I open a window, the ear-splitting squeal blessedly quits.

Several minutes later, I sit back down on the sofa, and scowl at the screen as I watch as my teammates try not to laugh.

"Cookies burnt to a crisp?" Ford asks with a smirk on his face.

"Yes." I sigh loudly.

"Do we need to end our video conference so you can call the fire department?" Jacob says, then slaps his leg and hoots.

I glower fiercely back at him. When all three of my colleagues double over, bursting out in loud guffaws, a grin reluctantly crosses my face. Within seconds, though, I'm pulled into the hilarity of the situation. "Guess Grandma Erma will . . . have to bake the cookies . . . for the church bake sale . . . since mine aren't fit to eat," I gasp out in spirts between cackles. We laugh for several minutes.

At least there's a silver lining to my baking failure, it makes everyone forget the discussion about Dad's visit. Once our merriment subsides, Jacob moves on to other topics. *If only it was that easy for my brain to accept Dad's reconciliation proposal.*

Chapter Twenty-Seven

Jacob

I'm half asleep when my phone rings. I squint at the alarm clock and it reads 2:15 am. Annoyed at the loud ringing, I almost turn it off and roll over. But my better judgement quickly takes over. This is the final countdown week for baby watch—Maybe Maddie's on her way to the hospital to deliver the twins.

"Hello," I croak out.

There's no response, but I think I hear low moans on the other end of the line. Still mostly asleep, I almost hang up, but first double check the screen. *Why is Daisy calling at this time of night?*

"Jacob." The voice on the other end of the line is so faint, I can barely hear it.

I press the phone firmer against my ear. "Daisy? Are you okay?"

When she doesn't reply, my voice gets louder. "Daisy! Talk to me. Are you okay?"

"No. I'm really sick . . . Gramps and Grandma are in Iowa." It sounds like she's crying. "Can you help me?"

I shoot to my feet, now fully awake. "Yes, I'm on my way. I'll be there as soon as I can." Throwing on a pair of blue jeans and a ratty sweatshirt, I grab my coat and keys and run out to my truck.

I drive the ten miles to her house like a maniac. My heart is racing as if it wants to escape the confines of my chest. She must be really sick to ask for help. Especially my help, after the way I've insisted that our relationship only be a professional one. I've berated myself for weeks over the dumb decision to be "friendly colleagues." Who am I kidding? I want Daisy with all my heart and not only as a colleague.

When I get to the carriage house, the only a light on is in the upstairs bathroom. I run to the front door.

Pound! Pound! Pound!

My fists rap against the door repeatedly, making enough noise to raise the neighbors who are five miles away. When I pause, I hear Mr. Bean yipping from somewhere inside. I wait several seconds, but there's no response. Knowing Daisy's first-rate security practices, I look under the Welcome mat for a key. Pulling out the shiny object, I unlock the door and rush inside.

I watch and listen for any movement, then I spot Mr. Bean at the top of the stairs. He's yipping and shaking his tiny body as if telling me to hurry up. I run up the stairs, taking them two at a time.

The master bedroom is empty, and the bed is unmade. Rumpled sheets indicate someone slept in it recently. I stride over to the master bathroom and push open the door. I find Daisy lying in a fetal position on the floor.

"Daisy, what's wrong?" I kneel beside her, putting my hand on her back. She's shaking and I hear her moan. Gently I roll her over so I can see her face. She's white like a sheet and there's a sheen of perspiration on her forehead. Her eyes are squeezed tightly shut. Her bright pink PJs are wrinkled as if she's worn them for several days.

"Little Bit, talk to me." I hope calling her that hated nickname will goad her into responding. Instead she draws her knees up further towards her chest, curling tightly into a ball.

I panic. Why won't she talk to me? I rub her arms and then pull her damp hair from her cheeks. She remains motionless and her mouth is pinched in pain. I stroke her cheeks. "Where does it hurt?" I bend closer so I'm talking directly into her ear.

Her eyes finally blink open. She pulls in a sharp breath and then groans. After a minute, she points to her lower right side. "Stabbing pain here. It won't go away . . ." She grimaces then

159

continues in a hesitant voice, "I'm nauseous . . . No food stays down . . ."

The effort to talk appears to be too much as her voice trails off and she closes her eyes again.

"Why didn't you call me sooner?" Her only response is to groan again in the back of her throat. Now is not a good time to scold her; at least she did finally call me. "Sweetheart, I'm going to pick you up. Then we're going to the hospital. Okay?"

She nods. I slip both my hands under her and pick her up. Her head falls limply against my chest. Another moan escapes her lips when I start to walk.

"I'm sorry if I'm hurting you." I try to not jostle her as I descend the stairs with her in my arms. Mr. Bean rushes ahead of us. I hear his toenails click on the wood floors as he runs to the front door.

"Mr. Bean, bed," I say in a firm, no nonsense voice and nod my head towards his bed in the corner. He runs over and plops down, putting his tiny head on his paws. His black eyes watch me all the way to the door.

"She's going to be fine." I wonder if I vocalize those words more to make myself feel better than to make the dog feel better.

Once outside, I carefully lay Daisy on the backseat in my truck. Her face is scrunched in obvious pain from me moving her, but she doesn't protest. I wish I had a blanket to put over her lightly clad body but I don't want to waste time looking for one. I'll crank up the heat in the truck and hope that keeps her warm.

Praying there's no traffic cops out at this time of night, I speed to the county hospital, running two red lights and ignoring three stop signs on the way. My heart is pounding in my chest and my hands are shaking. I look over my shoulder at the occupant of the backseat, but she hasn't moved a muscle since I put her there.

160

When we arrive at the hospital, I pull up to the emergency entrance. An attendant must be on watch, because he runs out when I jump from the truck. He runs over with a stretcher once he sees me lift Daisy from the backseat. I'm afraid she's passed out as her arms dangle limply at her sides.

"What's wrong with her?" the guy asks as he helps me shift Daisy onto the stretcher.

"She said she has a stabbing pain in her side." I motion to where she pointed earlier.

He nods, then starts to push her inside. "Park, then go to the reception desk and tell them you brought your wife into emergency and they'll direct you where to go." He disappears inside the sliding glass doors.

I don't correct him about the wife comment. They might not let me see her if I'm not next of kin.

The sleepy looking nurse at the reception desk points me down the hall to the emergency waiting area where another nurse meets me with a clipboard.

"Is it your wife in emergency?" she asks.

I shake my head, feeling too guilty to continue the misconception. "No, she's my girlfriend."

She scowls at me for a few seconds, then thrusts the clipboard into my hands. "Fill this out as best you can. How do we reach her next of kin?"

"They're out of town. I don't have their phone numbers. It's going to be difficult to reach them." Alec Montgomery's face pops into my mind, since technically he's her next of kin. I quickly discard the idea because I'm not sure whether Daisy would appreciate his involvement or not.

The nurse grunts and walks away, leaving me with the raft of paperwork. I sit in one of the plastic blue chairs in the empty waiting area and try to complete the forms, not knowing most of the answers. A pang of sadness hits me when I realize all the basic things I never bothered to learn about Daisy, like how tall she is and how much she weighs. Crabby Nurse is not going to like the incompleteness of my work.

When I walk over and hand the clipboard to her, she barely looks at me. I clear my throat. "Do they know what's wrong with my girlfriend?"

"The doctor said something about appendicitis. He'll come talk to you in a bit."

Realizing that I'm being dismissed, I return to the uncomfortable chair.

After what seems like an hour but may be only minutes, a man in green scrubs walks into the room. Since I'm the only person present, he makes a beeline for me, then sits in a chair across from mine.

"Hello. I'm Dr. Chen. Miss Montgomery needs emergency surgery. Her appendix burst and we need to remove it."

I feel sweat breakout on my forehead. "How risky is the surgery?" All I can think about are those medical dramas on TV where the patient has a minor surgery and dies. My heart drops to my toes.

"No need to worry. She's in good hands and the surgery is very routine. Since only next of kin can sign the release form, we're going ahead with the surgery without it." He reads something on his clipboard as I process his comment.

"Are you sure this is low risk? I'm the one who brought her in here, so I feel responsible."

Dr. Chen puts a reassuring hand on my arm. "Son, she's going to be fine. The surgery is very low risk."

I nod as he rushes off. Nothing bad can happen to Daisy—I haven't told her I love her yet. Even that hopeful thought doesn't help alleviate my anxiety.

My butt becomes numb after sitting in the waiting room for a couple of hours. Pulling out my cell phone, I see it's 5:30 am. My finger swipes to contacts and I place a call to Max, who's expecting me at a jobsite at 6.

"Hey, Jacob. What's up?"

My brother's friendly voice is like a lifeline. I'm so glad he answered.

"I'm at the hospital with Daisy." My voice cracks like a teenager. "Her appendix burst and she's in emergency surgery right now . . ."

He cuts off my words. "What? Is she going to be okay?"

"I don't know yet. No relative was here to sign the release form, so they just went ahead with the surgery. But I brought her here, what if that choice . . ." I gulp down the panic in my throat. "I'm praying that she's going to be okay."

"I'll let Luke know you won't be on the job this morning. Keep me posted about Daisy. And Jacob . . . I'm sure you did the right thing." His calm voice and reassurance make me feel a little better.

I click off and sit staring into space for a few minutes. Daisy is more than just a colleague. In fact, if I'm truthful with myself, I can't live without her. I'm in love with her. The realization of my feelings for her hits me like a slap in the face. I've been an idiot insisting that our relationship be only a professional one. I need to tell her how I feel as soon as possible.

About half an hour later, my brother Quinn strides in. I look up in surprise as he sits down next to me. "Why are you here?"

He pats my knee. "Max said you needed some moral support, so I'm here. I need to be in court by seven, but I can stay for a few minutes." Quinn hands me a take-out coffee container that I hadn't noticed in his hand. "Here, this will beat that crappy hospital coffee."

I take a sip, relieved that my brother is here to help me. "Thanks for coming. I was scared out of my mind for Daisy. She was in a lot of pain and didn't respond to much of what I said to her. Then the hospital went ahead with the surgery because no one was available to sign the consent form . . ." I shake my head, still questioning that decision.

Quinn nods. "Have faith, Jacob. She's a little fighter. I've never known a Vandervoldt to give up on anything."

That brings a partial smile to my face. She is half Vandervoldt, and that must count for something.

The exhaustion, adrenaline, and anxiety hit me all at once and make me want to come clean with all my feelings. Looking my brother in the eye, I say, "I have to admit I've always been a little in awe of you and Max. Always calm under pressure. Both successful businessmen. And here I am, a laid-off advertising manager turned construction worker." The words I've bottled up for several months just tumble from my mouth.

My brother's jaw drops, and he blinks at me. "What? Jacob, I never knew you felt this way."

I shrug. "Didn't you ever wonder why I didn't attend family gatherings very often? I was trying to make a name for myself at my old firm, so I prioritized company before family. Look how good that worked out. I'm a failure who had to come back home and live with his parents."

Quinn chuckles. "I feel your pain there, man." His expression turns serious. "None of us ever thought you were a failure. Max is so happy you're helping him out with the construction. And on top of that you start an advertising agency? Plus, you introduced the Big Brother organization to Connor's Grove. Little brother, you're impressive. Max and I should be in awe of you."

My eyes well up and a lump sits in my throat. After a couple seconds, I rasp out, "Thanks for telling me that. It means a lot." I feel like a weight's been lifted from my chest.

Slapping me on the back, Quinn says, "Okay, enough male bonding for one day. Let me show you some pictures of your niece."

Sipping my coffee, I listen while Quinn entertains me with the latest about baby Lilly and all her accomplishments such as sitting up, cutting a tooth, and even one attempt to crawl. His phone contains hundreds of photos, and the proud dad shows them to me even though I've seen them all before. I have to admit, the conversation is effective since it takes my mind and my worries off Daisy.

Just as Quinn is standing to leave, Dr. Chen walks in. Quinn says hello and shakes Dr. Chen's hand. They seem to know each other. My brother squeezes my shoulder, then leaves.

"Ah, so you're a Connor," Dr. Chen says once my brother has disappeared.

"Yes. Jacob Connor," I stand, and we shake hands.

"Your girlfriend came through surgery with flying colors. She's not awake yet. I'll have a nurse come get you when she wakes up and you can talk to her."

Relief spreads through my body. I sag back down into the blue chair because my knees no longer want to support me. "Thank you," I croak out as the doctor nods and exits.

Chapter Twenty-Eight

Daisy

Something smells awful—like antiseptic or cleaning supplies. I wrinkle my nose. Part of me wants to keep sleeping and part of me wants to wake up. I float between both states. After a few more seconds of semi-consciousness, my eyes fly open. *Where am I?*

Turning my head, I see monitors beeping and hissing. When I turn the other direction, I see Jacob sitting in a straight-backed chair positioned beside the bed. He smiles, stands, and takes my hand. "Are you feeling better?"

Memories of torturous pain come flooding back into my brain. When I touch the side of my body where the pain was, it feels numb. "What happened?" My brain is still a little fuzzy and I struggle to remember all the events leading up to this moment.

Jacob sits back down while continuing to hold my hand.

"I'm thirsty," I say before he has a chance to answer my question.

He smiles and reaches for a cup with a straw. He helps me put the straw in my mouth, and the cool water feels wonderful to my lips and parched throat. I drink a few sips and then motion for him to put the cup back down.

As if he can't resist touching me, Jacob gently pulls the hair back from my face. His thumb rubs my cheek as he looks at me. Tenderness and something else reflect in his eyes. I squint at him, trying to read what's on his mind.

"Your appendix burst, and Dr. Chen had to remove it. He'll be here in a few minutes to explain everything."

My eyes go wide. *No wonder I feel so out of it.* "I remember bits and pieces . . . The awful pain . . . You helping me." I blink at the unexpected tears trying to leak out of my eyes. *Why am I being so emotional?*

Jacob shifts to sit beside me on the bed. "You scared me to death, Daisy. I don't know what I'd do if I lost you."

The tears leak out of my eyes now. His words are so tender, and he looks like he wants to kiss me.

Jacob uses his thumb to wipe the tears from my face. "Why are you crying?"

I shake my head, unable to form words, as perplexed as he is as to the reason. This sweet, wonderful Jacob is melting my heart. No more businesslike Jacob—he's been replaced with the guy I was dating a few months ago.

"I had an epiphany while you were in surgery."

My eyes widen.

He pulls my hand he's holding to his lips and kisses it.

My eyes widen further.

"Daisy Montgomery, I knew from the first day that I met you that I loved you. I fell for you in that skimpy bikini and again when you wore those impractical shoes and again when you had the fishing rod in your hands . . ." He bends down and gently touches his lips to mine. "We've wasted enough time with my stupid declaration about business-only relationships."

I nod in agreement, my eyes as big as saucers. My heart soars because I can't believe what I'm hearing.

He gently takes my hand and places it over his heart. "You own my heart and my soul. How would you feel about taking our relationship to the next level?"

"You mean start dating again?" My voice is barely above a whisper, as if I might talk too loudly and break the spell between us.

He smiles and shakes his head. "I think we did that already."

I frown. "What do you mean, then?" My head hurts trying to read between the lines.

I feel his heartbeat knocking against my hand. His expression looks nervous yet determined. "Sweet, beautiful Daisy, will you marry me?"

I gasp as the tears leak out in force. I turn my head into his chest and blubber, "Yes, I'll marry you."

He laughs and his voice is ecstatic. "That better not just be the drugs talking, because we're getting married as soon as possible."

I rub the stubble on his cheek and nod. "I mean it with all my heart, and a clear head."

We gaze at each other for what could be seconds or minutes. Time has no meaning. The love in Jacob's eyes makes me feel cherished. When someone loudly clears their throat, we both turn towards the noise.

A doctor in green scrubs is hovering at the door. He strides into the room and holds his hand out to me. "I'm Dr. Chen." We shake, then he turns to Jacob. "This is my third time to witness a Connor marriage proposal in this hospital. How many more siblings do you have?"

We all laugh.

Chapter Twenty-Nine

Jacob

What a strange morning. My girlfriend has emergency surgery. I spill my guts to my brother. And I ask my girlfriend to marry me. Whew, that's a full day.

I walk towards the hospital exit with a sappy smile on my face. When I pass another one of the waiting rooms, I see Mom, Ash, Hailey, and Dad all sitting in a row. They're chatting and talking as if having a party. I stop and do a double take. Yep, that's the Connors.

"What are you all doing here?" I say as I walk into the room. *Did they come to check on Daisy?*

Collectively, they spring to their feet. "Jacob!" Mom wails in a loud voice. She pulls me into a tight hug as if she hasn't seen me in decades. The rest of the Connors are all talking at once.

"We tried to text you; did you not get it?" Ash asks.

Oops. I turned off my phone when I was sitting with Daisy and forgot to turn it back on.

"Is Daisy alright?" Hailey asks. Baby Lilly snuggles in her mom's arms while she looks at me with a smile that reveals the one tooth Quinn was so proud of.

"We're waiting for the twins to arrive," Dad says.

His words penetrate my brain. "Maddie's in labor?" I say excitedly.

Everyone nods.

"Her water broke about an hour ago. Max is back with her," Mom says. "Sit down, we expect it to be awhile."

I was planning on going home to take a shower, but instead I sit and join the baby arrival watch. Why not? Daisy's sleeping and I can't see her again for a couple of hours.

"Well, you never answered the question. How's Daisy?" Ash asks this time.

"You probably heard, her appendix burst and she had to have emergency surgery. It was very scary . . ." I pause as I remember the horrific events of earlier this morning. "She finally woke up just a few minutes ago. She's doing much better."

"That sweet girl. Lucky you were there for her," Hailey says with a wink.

"I guess you already know all the details from Quinn and Max?"

They nod.

"Is Quinn coming after he's done in court?" I ask while I debate whether to tell them the news about Daisy and me. Mom will start planning our wedding as soon as I tell her.

"He'll be here sometime after lunch. He's going to bring us food. I can call him and give him your order," my sweet sister-in-law says as she pulls out her cell phone.

"Sure, in a minute. I have some news to share." My words spill from my mouth before my brain can stop them.

Five pairs of eyes stare at me. Even baby Lilly seems interested in whatever I'm going to say.

My heart kicks up and I have to clear my throat in order to speak. "I asked Daisy to marry me and she said yes."

For the second time this morning, the Connors all surge to their feet. Mom squeals while Hailey makes the call on her phone to tell Quinn. Ash shakes her head, knowing she'll be the only remaining unmarried Connor sibling.

After a few minutes of celebrating, Dad says, "What is it about this hospital that makes the Connor men want to propose?"

Mom corrects him, "Maddie proposed to Max as you recall."

Dad grunts. "There's something in the water," he says, then sits back down and opens the *Field and Stream* he was reading. The rest of us snicker and Lilly claps her tiny hands.

~*~

We've consumed the lunch that Quinn brought from Crossroads Deli. It was like an in-hospital picnic for the Connors. Several nurses gave us the stink-eye for our boisterous party. Face it, my family knows how to have a good time.

I've played Candy Crush on my phone until my eyes are blurry. Dad's still poring over that old issue of *Field and Stream*. Mom, Ash, and Hailey are huddled, giggling and chatting in the corner, probably planning my wedding. Baby Lilly sits on Quinn's knee and chews on her chubby fist while her dad talks on his cell phone about some court case he's working on.

When are these twins going to arrive?

Just as that thought pops into my brain, Max strides in. His hair is mussed and the blue scrubs he's wearing barely fit his muscular frame. He looks happy but tired.

The Connors all rush to his side, anxious for the baby update.

"We have a healthy boy and a healthy girl!" He laughs, and cheers ring out across the group. "It was a big surprise since the doctor told us we were having two girls." Max and Maddie had not revealed the gender, so this is news to everyone.

"Is Maddie doing okay?" Hailey asks. Being a new mom herself, she knows just what went down in the delivery room.

Max winces. "She's a little disappointed because they had to deliver the babies by C-section because her labor just wasn't progressing like it should." He shakes his head and looks over the group. "Everything happened so fast, I couldn't come tell you. Thankfully Maddie and the babies are doing fine."

Relief spreads across everyone's face.

171

"What do they weigh?" Ash asks.

Max smiles proudly. "The boy is five pounds six ounces and the girl five pounds even."

Mom nudges Max in the side. "What did you name them?"

My brother smiles. "We had the names all decided for two girls. They were going to be Faith and Hope. But neither of those names translates too well for a boy."

The crowd murmurs their agreement.

Max continues. "Maddie still wants to use the name Faith. She said that my faith in us finally getting together is a blessing and she's thankful every day that I didn't give up." He pauses and blinks a few times, emotion clearly showing on his weary face. It was a rocky road, but Max finally won her over.

Mom, Hailey and Ash all wipe tears from their eyes after that speech. Dad blows his nose loudly. Quinn and I exchange grins.

"What did you name the boy?" Quinn asks after our brother doesn't continue with his story.

"Oh yeah. We decided on Wyatt. That was Maddie's dad's middle name. Wyatt Quinton is his full name."

Max turns to Quinn and they share a brotherly hug. The two men look teary eyed when they pull apart.

"So, what's Faith's middle name?" Ash inquires. She always wants all the details.

"Faith Catherine after Nana."

Oohs and aahs echo around the room. Nana is beloved to everyone in the family.

"I'll call Nana right away and tell her," Mom says excitedly as she walks over to a quiet corner.

"She's probably playing Pinochle," Dad says in an overly loud voice, knowing Mom has already tuned everyone out.

I walk over to my brothers. Max pulls me into a quick hug. I can't believe both brothers are now fathers.

"Jacob has some news," Quinn says as he winks at me.

Max raises his eyebrow.

A huge smile splits my face. "Daisy and I are getting married."

"Way to go Jacob!" Max says as he high-fives me, then follows with another brotherly hug.

When Max turns back to Quinn, my brothers both chuckle, knowing the location where we're standing and the Connor brothers' history here.

Max breaks up the party. "I'll let you know when the twins are in the nursery and you can go see them. And I'll tell Maddie your news, Jacob." He strides back down the hall.

That's also my cue to go see my fiancée.

"I'm going to visit Daisy again and tell her about the twins," I say as I walk quickly down the hall towards her room. She'll be excited, and maybe we can go visit the babies together.

Chapter Thirty

Daisy

I stare at the gorgeous ring Jacob bought me. He asked if I wanted to go with him to pick it out, but I preferred it be a surprise. He outdid himself with a vintage style that has a center marquise diamond surrounded by other tiny diamonds. We reenacted the proposal scene in my carriage house, where Jacob got down on one knee while Mr. Bean tried to lick his face. I laughed so hard it felt like I might rupture my stitches.

"So, fiancée, when and where are we getting married? I can't hold Mom off for another day. She needs the details," Jacob says with a chuckle as we sit on my sofa. He watches over me like a hawk and waits on me hand and foot. I'm getting a bit spoiled.

Biting my lip, I turn towards him. "I have a weird proposal, so hear me out."

My beloved rolls his eyes as if he's used to my off-the-wall ideas. He takes my hand and kisses it, trying to distract me.

"No touching until I get this out. You scramble my brain," I say as I pull my hand out from under his lips.

He gives me a smirk but keeps his hands to himself. I have his full attention.

"Mr. Bean and I used to go to weddings," I say.

Jacob raises his eyebrows and looks between me and my dog. "You and Beanie were wedding crashers?"

I giggle and elbow him. "No, silly, not that Mr. Bean."

Mr. Connor nods. "Ah, the other Mr. Bean."

"Right. Mr. Bean was a wedding attendant. He stood up as a witness when a couple didn't have anyone else. Or he walked the bride down the aisle. He worked at one of the chapels on the strip. We sat in the pews and waited to see if he was called on. I was only eight or nine years old, but I fell in love with the beautiful dresses, flowers, and all the pomp and circumstance. I attended hundreds of weddings with Mr. Bean, and I would always imagine myself in them—"

Jacob holds up his hand to stop the flow of my words. "Are you saying you want to get married in Vegas?"

"Exactly. The chapel where Mr. Bean worked is beautiful. The best thing is, we can get married next week. No big fuss, no huge party to plan. Easy, peasy." I make a dusting motion with my hands.

My fiancé looks a little skeptical. "Mom's going to be very disappointed. Everyone will think that we had to get married." He looks at my tiny waistline and his words sink in, causing me to blush.

"Um, I didn't consider that part . . . Well, when a baby doesn't come along in nine months, I guess they'll know the truth."

He's still not convinced, by the look on his face. "Won't your Gramps and Grandma want to throw you a big wedding?"

"Jacob, you do remember how big the Vandervoldt family is? They've had their fair share of weddings by now. Plus, we'll have a big party when we get home. Your mom and Grandma Erma can go all out. We'll invite all the Connors and Vandervoldts in the tri-county area."

Jacob laughs. "You're a Vegas girl after all, aren't you?"

I nod. "Born and raised."

"I agree on one condition," Mr. Connor says while giving me a firm look.

"Okay, what's your condition?"

He smirks. "You tell Mom."

~*~

Ford and Sylvie insist on coming with us to Vegas. They call it a Cherry on Top company policy to support their colleagues. I personally think it's an excuse to gamble.

"This bridal boutique rocks," Sylvie squeals as we look at wedding dresses.

I thought it would be easier to purchase one here, but after looking through the racks, these dresses all look quite expensive. Guess they have a captive audience and can charge whatever they want.

"May I help you?" A tall blonde saunters up, looking like a fashion model. Every hair is perfectly groomed and she's wearing an expensive-looking suit. *Not a good sign for my budget.*

"She needs a wedding dress by tomorrow," my friend excitedly explains.

"Well, that doesn't leave much time for alterations," the blonde says in a snooty voice while looking at me as if they have nothing in my size.

I wrinkle my nose but follow her to a back room with racks and racks of dresses.

"These are our off-the-rack collection. Find your size and let me know if you want to try anything on." She disappears as if we're not worthy of her time.

"She's snotty, isn't she?" Sylvie says as we look through size four dresses.

I huff but continue looking. After scouring the racks for thirty minutes, I'm about ready to give up hope. Maybe I can find something at Target.

Sylvie tugs on a dress that's hidden behind another dress. She pulls and pulls, finally revealing a knee-length creation. "What do you think of this one?"

I join her and hold the dress up to me. Turning to the full-length mirror at the end of the rack, we both stare at the lovely dress. It's an off-the-shoulder white silk with a tight waist and full skirt. A rhinestone encrusted belt circles the waist, but it looks elegant rather than cheesy.

We exchange smiles in the mirror.

"It'll need hemming," I say in a hesitant voice.

"Well, if Miss Congeniality can't get it hemmed by tomorrow, then she loses the sale. End of discussion."

I laugh at my red-headed friend's strong words. "Let's go try it on."

Sylvie rushes off to find the blonde. I stare at the dress, knowing it's perfect.

~*~

I insist on the traditional wedding march song. It plays from a DVD player sitting in the corner. The tiny speakers don't produce the best sound, but at least we have music. I walk down the slightly wrinkled red-carpet runner on the arm of a distinguished-looking gray-haired gentleman who reminds me a little of Mr. Bean. A twinge of sadness stabs me in the chest because I wish the real Mr. Bean were here with me. I imagine his wrinkled face, shock of white hair, and ram-rod straight stature. Although he's no longer with us, he still lives in my heart.

Jacob and Ford are standing at the altar that's embellished with red and white roses. I don't look too closely because I suspect the flowers are fake. Both men look like a million bucks in their black tuxes. Sylvie stands on the other side in a recycled bridesmaid dress from a previous wedding she was in. She looks beautiful in the emerald green color because it shows off her creamy white skin and red hair perfectly. Ford can't keep his eyes off her. *Is there another wedding in store for Cherry on Top?*

Once I get to the front of the chapel, Jacob takes my hand. He's beaming, and his tender smile causes my heart to do a double somersault and triple flip with the skill of an Olympic gymnast.

"You look breathtaking," he whispers to me, making me blush. My skin probably looks like a lobster against the pure white dress.

The officiant draws our attention as he reads the exchange of vows. The whole process takes only a few minutes. We went with the budget-friendly "timeless" ceremony. No live performance of a love song (done by the owner's daughter), no poetry reading (by same daughter), and no bouquets or boutonnieres for the bridal party. Jacob and I giggled at all the upselling that the owner's daughter tried to do, especially the parts of the ceremony that she would get paid for. But, the man to walk me down the aisle, an officiant to read the vows, tux rental, and a complimentary glass of champagne came with this economy package.

I felt a little pang of guilt that a stranger will be walking me down the aisle since I'm trying to forge a relationship with my dad. Even though we've made strides to get to know each other, I just don't feel comfortable enough with him yet to invite him into something this private.

When Jacob hears the words "You may kiss the bride," he lifts me off my feet and kisses the breath right out of my body. I feel the kiss all the way to my toes. Ford and Sylvie clap, and the guy who walked me down the aisle gives me a wink.

"Congratulations!" The owner's daughter appears, dressed in a fancy red gown, and hands out the complimentary glasses of champagne.

"To the new couple," Ford says in his booming voice. "May you have happiness, prosperity and enough kids to field a baseball team."

"What?" I say with a look of horror on my face. I look sternly at my new husband. "We didn't negotiate that, Mr. Connor."

Jacob grins and waggles his eyebrows. "It'll be fun trying. Vandervoldts have big families."

I roll my eyes.

The four of us clink our glasses together despite Ford's lame toast. As we sip the bubbly drink, the owner's daughter snaps a photo on her cell phone. "No extra charge. Just give me your email address and I'll send this to you." *Well, how generous of her.*

Since the next wedding starts in ten minutes, we collect our official wedding license issued by the state of Nevada and signed by our officiant before we book it out of there. I can't wait to get out of these high heels.

At the chapel door, Jacob pauses and gently takes me into his arms. His gorgeous blue eyes stare into my chocolate brown ones as if he can see all the way into my soul. "I love you, Mrs. Connor."

I stand on my toes and we share a lingering kiss. "I love you too, Mr. Connor. With all my heart."

The unlovable girl finally found someone who'll love her forever. Someday is today.

Chapter Thirty-One

Jacob

Mom's been driving Daisy and me crazy for the two weeks since our Vegas wedding. Her idea of a wedding reception party is much different than ours. After several rounds of trying to whittle down the invitee list, Daisy succumbs and lets Mom do whatever she wants. Even if she doesn't know when to stop, Mom's heart is in the right place.

"What time do we have to be at your parents' house?" Daisy asks in a distracted voice. She's in the corner painting and, as usual, has lost track of time.

I wander over to look at progress on the painting. Leaning in, I kiss her neck while she giggles and breaks out in goose bumps.

"Is that the chapel where we got married?"

My wife turns in my arms. "Yes, I want to remember every moment of our beautiful ceremony."

The painting is a scene, with two figures holding hands at the front of a chapel. She's captured the rose-covered altar and the long red runner extending down the aisle perfectly. The way the male figure is gently holding the female figure's hand as he slides the ring on her finger gives the viewer a sense that the couple is enamored with each other. I don't know how Daisy does it, but she painted our love into this picture. My eyes fill with tears just looking at it.

I shake my head and sniffle, trying to wipe the tears away before she sees them.

"Mr. Connor, are you getting emotional over my painting?" Daisy asks with awe in her voice.

Nodding, I put my lips on hers, trying to express how I feel through a kiss because mere words will never be enough. My heart is filled with passion, devotion, and love for this beautiful woman with a big attitude.

After several minutes, Daisy pulls back and whispers, "What time did you say we need to be there?"

I glance at the clock on the microwave. "We have thirty minutes to get ready and get there."

"What?" My wife scrambles to put her paints away. We're going to be late to our own party. I chuckle.

~*~

The party room at the community center is decorated with silver bells, red crepe paper streamers, and white tablecloths. Very elegant, even if these were the only decorations readily available near Christmas. This was the only place big enough to contain Mom's extensive guest list on such short notice. She greets us at the door while our seventy-five guests mingle and wait for us. It's a huge gathering by Connor's Grove standards.

Daisy clutches my hand firmly as if she needs a lifeline to get through this. I know her dislike of crowds, but she's already met many people who are coming today. Except for some far flung relatives like Great-Aunt Gertrude and Great-Uncle Willard who Mom insisted should be invited (and who apparently give nice gifts).

"Look who's finally arrived," Mom says in a deafening voice. A hush settles over the gathering as everyone turns and we walk in. After a few seconds, the crowd begins to clap and cheer. My wife blushes while I hold our clasped hands up over my head as if I won first place at the county fair. Which I did—a prize so precious that I'm going to treasure her every day of my life.

Connors and Vandervoldts patiently wait as Mom acts like a drill sergeant, directing everyone to form a line so they can greet us in an orderly fashion. Daisy and I stand at the front of the room.

Our guests will give their well wishes, then grab a plate and go through the buffet line. Leave it to Mom to make everything so efficient.

Quinn and Hailey greet us first. A sleepy-looking baby Lilly rest her head on her dad's shoulder. She's going to be out like a light very soon.

"Congratulations, Brother," Quinn says as he pulls me into a bear hug while trying not to squish the baby.

"You look stunning," Hailey says to my wife as she admires Daisy's festive red dress which fits her like a glove. I'm going to enjoy removing that later.

The women hug and wipe tears at the same time. Quinn steps forward to hug Daisy, then pulls his dawdling wife along as they head to the buffet table.

I spot Max and Maddie at the other side of the room. This is their first party since the birth of the twins. They can hardly move around the room with all the oohing and aahing over the babies. Faith and Wyatt are both growing like weeds, and their parents, while tired from lack of sleep, look happier than I've ever seen them. Daisy and Maddie exchange smiles and finger waves. The sisters-in-law bond grew stronger when the babies were born since Maddie and Daisy were both in the hospital at the same time. Max gestures at us over the crowd and mouths, "We'll catch you two later."

I laugh and nod in response to my brother.

Daisy whispers in my ear, "Once we've seen everyone, I'm going to go hold Faith or Wyatt. I can't wait to see how much they've grown." She fell in love with the babies while she was in the hospital and visited them every day.

Ash grabs my arm, getting my attention. She pulls both Daisy and me into a hug. My little sister is rather shy even though she has a big mouth. She seems speechless as she smiles at me.

182

"Hey, Ash, I'll even try some of your healthy salad without protest today," I tease. My sister punches me in the arm at that comment.

When John and Erma walk up, the waterworks begin. Daisy sobs as Gramps pulls her into a hug. Grandma Erma takes out a tissue from her purse and wipes the tears from Daisy's face. It takes a few minutes for everyone to get their emotions back under control.

"Kiddo, you did good," Gramps says while smiling at his granddaughter.

He turns to me and firmly shakes my hand. "I trust you to love her as much as Grandma and I do." I nod and wipe a few tears from my eyes, as does the tall gentleman.

A man who's been hovering in the background walks up. I smile internally when I see that it's Alec Montgomery. His pristine tailor-made suit and shined shoes look a little out of place on a Saturday.

He shakes my hand, then turns to Daisy. She's biting her lip as she looks hesitantly at her dad. "Congratulations, Daisy. I wouldn't miss being here on your special day." He pauses, blinks a few times, and clears his throat. "I hope that we can see each other often and that we can finally put the past behind us."

My sweet wife hugs her father, then wipes more tears away as she says, "I'd like that Dad."

The formidable Mr. Montgomery looks like he has a few tears on his face as well.

When he walks away, Daisy says directly into my ear, "Did you invite him?"

I nod. "I asked Mom to include him, but I wasn't sure whether he would come."

My wife squeezes my arm with tears still in her eyes. "Thank you."

When Ford and Sylvie walk up, Daisy squeals as if she hasn't seen them in years. Ford and I chuckle at the ladies' enthusiasm. They hug and giggle for several minutes while us guys stand awkwardly in the background.

"Come on Sylvie, let's get some food," Ford finally says and drags her away. The big man is always hungry.

Relatives from near and far walk up to greet us. The line moves slowly as we reconnect with cousins, aunts, and uncles—or we meet distant relatives for the first time (and yes, Gertrude and Willard are quite charming, and so spry for their age). After greeting everyone, I think Mom invited every Connor she's ever known. Even the Vandervoldts are here en masse.

After we've greeted everyone, Mom and Dad appear. Mom sniffles and hugs Daisy and I. Dad even has a few tears, but he's much less demonstrative than Mom.

"Nana and Grandad send their love. We'll have a family dinner when they return from Florida so they can meet your lovely wife," Mom says.

Daisy and I nod.

"Mrs. Connor, thank you for the beautiful party. It was so thoughtful of you," Daisy says.

"My dear, call me Jeannie. And it was my pleasure. Obviously, my son is head over heels in love with you. I can't wait for more grandbabies!" She says with a wink that causes Daisy to blush to the roots of her hair.

Dad points to the buffet table. "Better get some food before I hit the buffet." Mom smacks him in the arm.

Daisy giggles as I lead her to get some of the delicious food. As usual, Mom cooked enough to feed half the town. My gorgeous bride picks up a plate, then whispers, "I love the Connors, especially their youngest son."

I kiss her cheek. "Don't forget to get some of Grandma Erma's German chocolate cake. You won my heart when you baked one for me." I point towards the ravaged cake at the end of the table. There's only one piece remaining.

My wife smiles. "A wise woman told me that a way to a man's heart is through his stomach."

I nod, knowing that all the Connor and Vandervoldt women believe that to be true. And maybe it is.

Epilogue

Daisy — Six Months Later

It's so peaceful here. Since Jacob moved into the carriage house, we go fishing at least once a week if the weather cooperates. Today is a perfect day for fishing—not too hot, and the lake looks like glass.

My husband still teases me about the fact that I bait my own hook. I've also seen him practicing his casting in the backyard. His competitive nature doesn't like the fact that I still out-cast him.

I bite my lip in concentration as I put the slimy night crawler on the hook. My husband laughs as he watches me. I turn towards him, sticking out my tongue. Mr. Bean sits at my feet, debating whether to sit by me or Jacob, knowing that we will both spoil him with treats.

I cast, then settle into the lawn chair that my devoted husband lugged all the way out here. He casts and moves his chair closer to mine. When he sits down, he takes my hand and intertwines our fingers. We sit like this for minutes as we watch the red and white bobbers bounce in the water.

My latest Cherry on Top design tumbles around in my brain as we relax. "Do you mind if I ask a couple questions about the next Montgomery Enterprises project? I need clarification on a couple items."

My husband raises his eyebrows. I've caught him by surprise.

"My dear, I usually don't mix business and pleasure. Can your questions wait until Monday?"

I grin and shake my head at his response. "Well, I might not be able to match the aggressive deadlines that our project manager put in place if I don't get my technical questions answered soon."

Said project manager tsks and points to the lake. "Woman, focus on your fishing. Grandma Erma is having a fish fry if we can catch enough."

I giggle, then remember the topic I wanted to ask while my husband is relaxed and chilling out. "Well, if you want to talk about pleasure instead of business . . . Remember when I said you owe me for keeping my mouth shut to Max about the smelly paint incident? I'm finally calling in my marker."

My husband rolls his eyes. "Do you really need *more shoes*?"

A belly laugh escapes. "No, that's not my request."

"Um, let me think. You want me to pose in the buff so you can paint me? I'm in for that, by the way."

I groan. "Jacob, be serious. Where would we hang a painting like that?"

He smirks. "In the master bedroom, for inspiration?"

A warmth creeps up my neck and cheeks. My husband can still make me blush. But I'm not going to let him distract me. "I want a buddy for Mr. Bean."

"Oh, like a Mrs. Bean?"

Nodding, I say, "Pretty much. I went to the Chihuahua Rescue yesterday and found a cute female who will make Mr. Bean so happy. Can I adopt her?"

Mr. Connor sighs. "Daisy Mae, you know I can't say no to you."

Smiling, I squeeze his hand. "We'll go get her tomorrow. Mr. Bean will be so excited."

"I think it's Mrs. Connor who will be so excited, but who I am I to argue with my sweet wife?"

I roll my eyes at his words.

We sit in companionable silence. The gentle breeze and soothing sound of the water lapping at the shore make me almost fall asleep. I feel myself drifting off when . . .

Whirr! Whirr!

The tug nearly pulls the rod from my hand as the line unwinds from the reel. I squeal and stand. "I've got a big one."

Mr. Bean yips at the excitement. My husband joins me with a net in his hand, ready to land my big fish.

Pulling and reeling, I feel the fish fight me every inch of the way. I use both hands and all my strength, but I feel like I'm gaining on him. Eventually we see the fish at the end of the line as he surfaces, and I continue to reel him in. Once he's close to the shore, Jacob scoops him up in the net.

"A walleye pike. Nice job." He holds the net with my squirming fish up so I can see it.

"Can we weigh him?"

Jacob laughs, knowing how competitive I am. My husband currently holds the record for largest fish caught in the lake, but this one looks like a contender for the crown. "Of course, sweetie. When we get home, I'll have Gramps weigh him before we clean him."

I wrinkle my nose. Cleaning fish is something I avoid. Fortunately, the men in my life are happy to do it.

Jacob puts the fish on ice in the cooler. It joins the other three white bass that my man caught earlier. We sit back down in our chairs. I lay my rod on the ground beside me.

"That guy pooped me out. I'll watch while you fish."

My husband nods, casts, and motions for Mr. Bean to jump in his lap. My spoiled dog happily obliges.

"Hailey, Maddie, Ash, and I are having lunch on Monday. I can't wait to see the twins and Lilly."

"Tell the ladies hello from me, and give the babies a kiss."

I nod. "I just love those little guys." I watch the expression on my husband's face closely, trying to gauge his reaction.

He smiles. "Me too."

I wait a couple seconds debating with myself. *Is this the time to tell him?* Finally, I blurt out, "Would you mind terribly if I'm pregnant?"

Jacob drops his fishing rod, jumps to his feet, and pulls me from my chair. Mr. Bean yips a small protest at being dumped unceremoniously on the ground. Blue eyes stare intently at me. "Really?"

I giggle. "Really."

We kiss and hug for quite a few minutes. My hair is mussed and I'm breathless when my husband finally releases me. He gently rubs my stomach. "When did you find out?"

Blushing, I reply. "I got one of those tests from the pharmacy and did it yesterday. You know the one where you pee on a stick?" When my nose crinkles at the memory of me trying to aim for the tiny stick, my husband chuckles. "I was waiting for the perfect time to tell you."

"What makes fishing at the lake the perfect time to tell me?" He tilts up my chin and kisses me gently on the lips.

"It's our spot. I told you my horrendous life story the first time we came here."

He nods. "True."

"There must be something about the fresh air and the water that makes me want to spill the beans."

Jacob laughs. "So, if I ever want to know how much you spent on a pair of shoes, I bring you here?"

I punch him in the arm.

When we sit back down, Jacob picks up the discarded rod. Luckily, he didn't get a bite while we were distracted. Mr. Bean wisely stays sitting at my feet in case of another unexpected announcement.

"Mrs. Connor?"

I look over at my soulmate. "Yes, Mr. Connor?"

"You're the best thing that ever happened to me. I want you more and more each day. I'll never get enough of you."

"Good thing because I'm not going anywhere."

My love holds my hand and we sit watching the waves lap the shore. This is heaven on earth.

THE END

Note to Readers

Dear Reader—thank you for reading Book Three in my Connor Brothers series. If you like small town romances and Hallmark movies, you'll love this series of clean and wholesome romances.

I hope Daisy and Jacob's story brought you many hours of happiness, some laughs, and maybe a few tears. While Connor's Grove is a fictitious community, there are small towns all over America where neighbors care about each other and help when times are tough.

I have fond memories of living in Minnesota for fifteen years. Hopefully I captured some things that make Minnesotans special—their gusto for the sport of curling or fishing at a country lake, the Minnesota accent (sentence ending eh's), showing love through food such as Gloria sharing her award-winning brownies or Grandma Erma baking her famous German chocolate cake.

And, of course, the small town setting is perfect to show the strong bonds of family and community—a place where everyone has each other's back.

Ashleigh and Brock's story (Book 4 in the Connor Brothers series) is coming in Fall 2020. Plus, Sylvie and Ford are getting their own Christmas novella available in October. Please follow me on my website, Facebook, or Amazon author page or subscribe to my newsletter to be informed about upcoming book releases. Links to all of those are included in the "About the Author" chapter below.

Thank You and Happy Reading!

About the Author

Leah Busboom wanted to become an author since the day she learned how to read. She specializes in the romance genre because she loves a sweet love story with a happy ending. Her books are known for their heartwarming stories, intriguing characters, and hilarious real-life situations that will make you want to laugh out loud.

Leah currently lives in Colorado with her wonderful husband, her "Blue Bomber" bicycle, and a hundred bunny rabbits that roam free in the neighborhood.

Find out about Leah's latest book releases, sales and giveaways:

- AuthorLeahBusboom.com
- Newsletter Sign-up
- Leah Busboom Facebook Author Page
- Amazon Author Page

Books by Leah Busboom:

(all available on Amazon.com)

Chance on Love Series Trilogy:

- *Second Chances*—Matt and Samantha's story (Book 1)
- *Taking Chances*—Danny and Paige's story (Book 2) (Winner: 2018 Rocky Mountain Cover Art Contest— Sweetest Cover)
- *Lasting Chances*—Gabe and Megan's story (Book 3)
- Chance on Love Series Boxed Set – Books 1-3 in Chance on Love series

Unlikely Catches Series Trilogy:

- *Catching Cash's Heart*—Holly and Cash's story (Angel Wings & Fastballs) (Book 1)
- *Stealing Alan's Heart*—Brianna and Alan's story (Stilettos & Spreadsheets) (Book 2)
- *Winning Trey's Heart*—Abby and Trey's story (Playboy & the Bookworm) (Book 3)
- *Unwrapping Sam's Heart* – Lynn and Sam's story (A Christmas Novella) (Prequel to Book 1)
- *Melting Nick's Heart* – Bethany and Nick's story (A Valentine's Day Novella) (Sequel to Book 3)

Connor Brothers Series:

- Finding You – Quinn and Hailey's story (Book 1)
- Loving You – Max and Maddie's story (Book 2)
- Wanting You – Jacob and Daisy's story (Book 3)

Made in United States
Orlando, FL
22 July 2023

35381233R00107